Praise for

The Happenstances

AT THE YELLOW COUNTY COMMUNITY COLLEGE A COUPLE OF SEMESTERS LATER

"Heartwarming and hilarious tales of friendship that unfold at a blistering pace, the second book in *The Happenstances* . . . series is such a remarkable feat of young adult fiction that all I can say is: Dive in!"

—Joe McGinniss Jr.,
Author of *The Delivery Man* and *Carousel Court*

"I would read an entire encyclopedia if Peter Harmon penned the prose. His witty way with words will have you chuckling and smiling with every turn of the page. The happenstances tucked away in this beautifully wordsmith-ed creation make for a perfect summer read.

Get ready to dog-ear this book again and again because as Pete says: 'a dog-ear is a promise—hold my spot; I'll be back with reinforcements as soon as I can.' And this is a book that should be read as soon as you can!"

—Brittany Raschdorf, **Author of *The Hypnotist's Daughter***

"Harmon clearly had a blast creating this heartfelt and charming ode to summer love and witty wordplay, and the fun is infectious! I'd dog-ear every page that made me smile, but it would bend the whole book."

—Andrew Adams,
Creator/writer Schismatic and Revisionaries

"Did you ever want to go back in time—re-live a special moment with your closest friends? Well Peter Harmon has done just that, or at least he has created a time that should have been for a slightly off kilter, deftly drawn cast of characters who inhabit the suburban community of Yellow County.

In this, his second in the series, Harmon reunites the crew from the Yellow County Community Swim & Racquet Club as they enter their adult years and takes them on a dizzying journey of self-discovery through occasionally bizarre but unfailingly funny plot twists and turns.

The characters will be familiar to you, even if you haven't read Harmon's first book—which by all means you should. They are a well-conceived caricature of the kids we grew up with, and they live on in what we can all hope will be a third and fourth and many more adventures."

—Douglas A. Weiss, Author of *Life, Love & Internet Dating*

"The fun characters you know and love are back! Harmon knows how to bring a story to life, with his wit and vivid storytelling this summer read will have you hooked from the start."

—Jennifer & Hannah, TurnsMyPage

"Get ready to hit the ground reading as all your favorite wacky, unpredictable and forever lovable characters return, a few years older and yet hilariously not-all-that-wiser!

Harmon's witty wordplay and refreshing new take on breaking fourth walls allows us to join arms with our endearingly well-intentioned misfits—together finding love, fighting inner demons and ultimately striving to discover happiness in all of life's happenstances."

—Jamie Petitto, Digital Media Producer

The Happenstances
at the Yellow County Community College
a Couple of Semesters Later

by Peter L. Harmon

© Copyright 2017 Peter L. Harmon

ISBN 978-1-63393-439-9

Published by

◄ köehlerbooks™

210 60th Street
Virginia Beach, VA 23451
800-435-4811
www.koehlerbooks.com

The Happenstances

AT THE YELLOW COUNTY COMMUNITY COLLEGE
A COUPLE OF SEMESTERS LATER

THE 2ND BOOK IN THE HAPPENSTANCES...SERIES

PETER L. HARMON

VIRGINIA BEACH
CAPE CHARLES

DEDICATION

The first book in *The Happenstances* . . . series is dedicated to my wife Ashlea, my son Christian, and my friends and family who support my writing.

This book, the second in *The Happenstances* . . . series, is dedicated to everyone who has read the first book. If you love the characters of Yellow County half as much as I do, you're going to have some fun reading this story.

And also to my younger son, Calvin, who didn't make the cut the first time around. A good bit of this book was written during the months leading up to and right after he was born. I would put him in the baby carrier and stand at my desk and write while Ash would put Christian to bed or do chores or take some time for herself after a long day of being a little baby's mommy—one of the harder gigs out there, if you ask me.

So anyway, Cal Cal, I love you. Christian, you're my little big guy. Ash, thank you. (Summer, you know you're my favorite, but don't tell anyone.)

PROLOGUE

THE YELLOW COUNTY Community College of Yellow County, Maryland, was originally supposed to be a prison. It was intended to be the East Yellow County Correctional Facility, to be more precise. Midway through construction, the script was flipped, and the campus that was meant to confine and rehabilitate Yellow County's criminals was reimagined, rezoned, and revamped. The campus was then meant to confine and *educate* Yellow County's junior collegiate students. The thought was that a place of learning would quell the need for a place of imprisonment, Lord willing.

When the powers that be made the decision, the dining hall was already built for the prison, so that was a plus; not much needed to be changed in that regard. A shipment of convict gruel was already ordered, so when it came the head chef dubbed it "vegan goulash" and served it to the unsuspecting community college herbivores. The junior college vegan community was sparse, but luckily, they were usually very hungry and their taste buds were none too discriminating. They managed to polish off what the dining staff secretly referred to as "gruel-ash" pretty quickly. Nobody seemed certain what was in it.

A fairly charming chapel had been constructed on the sprawling lawn, or "yard" as it was referred to, and three walls of one of the main cell blocks were already up, which is the reason why three sides of the Yellow County Community College Library lack windows.

Even the solitary confinement basement was slickly repurposed to be what the administration referred to as "solo study cubicles." The bank of payphones for calls to lawyers and loved ones was rebranded "the hall of forgotten technology."

Once that whole snafu was de-snaffed, the rest of the construction of the Y-triple-C went relatively smoothly. Buildings named after great Yellow Countians of the past were erected. There was The Wittles Performing Arts Center next to the library, the Wilkenshire Facility west of the quad, and Grant Hill Hall over on Grant Hall's hill.

The crown jewel of the campus—the reason why students commuted from as far as Chevy Chase or even Brown Town— was the YCCC Indoor Pool and Fitness Facility. They moved weightlifting paraphernalia intended to pump up the prospective prisoners inside of the massive, many-windowed structure that housed the college's gymnasium. The facility donned a sauna, aquatic center, juice bar, indoor tetherball arena, trampoline park, and for some reason a fully functioning Dave & Buster's, where the tickets that you won playing the arcade-style games could be used as tender at the campus book store.

The swim team was renowned. For a community college, Yellow County was the winningest in the tri-county area—so good, in fact, that they were bumped up a couple of divisions and competed against four-year state colleges like Towson University and Brown State, the latter with whom there was a bitter rivalry. Brown Staters and YCCC-ites routinely sabotaged each other's campuses, with mostly harmless shenanigans like painting the dean's car brown or dying the practice pool's water yellow. One year, a trio of co-eds from YCCC even stole Brown State's mascot, Bernie the Brown State Brown Recluse; the abductors painted poor Bernie yellow. Bernie didn't play along; he bit the YCCC intruders, who all had to be medevacked to Prince George's hospital center for treatment for their oozing spider bites. In retaliation, some Brown Staters anonymously sent laxative brownies to their college apartment. The three pranksters thought it was a gift from sympathizers and took the bait. They spent the next few days scurrying to the toilet.

The YCCC Indoor Pool and Fitness Facility was still the mecca for community college-level swim meets. Those boys and girls on the YCCC swim team would really get to swimming. The bleachers were always packed with yellow-painted faces waving their yellow foam fingers formed into the sign for *Y* in sign language, which was often confused with the *hang loose* hand gesture. They would chant one of their trademark chants like, *"I swam across, I swam across for you. Oh what a thing to do, 'Cause the pool is all Yellow!"* or *"Yellow, it's YCC, I was wondering if after all these years you'd like to lose a swim meet."* And when that indoor pool was a-rockin', all were invited to come a-knockin' for a spectacular sports experience in a premiere natatorium.

The indoor pool had vaulted ceilings to accommodate the diving platforms. Blue-tinted windows let in cool light that shimmered off the water. A Maryland flag and an American flag hung on the wall. Names of prestigious swimmers also graced the walls with plaques that, from a distance, looked like a mouthful of unbrushed teeth.

If former lifeguard Jonathan Poole had once felt at home at the Yellow County Community Swim and Racquet Club (and then subsequently made it into his home for a spell) then this facility was an apt stand-in, if not replacement, for the pool where he had secretly lived a couple of semesters previous.

CHAPTER 1

FADE IN... was typed on a blank document on a computer screen. The cursor blinked like a bleary-eyed cave dweller, just come up to the Earth's surface for his or her first glimpse at the sun.

And blinked.

There was a sigh from Charlie Heralds, a handsome but shaggy and unshaven early twenty-something, as he sat at his computer in his small cluttered apartment. His *Animaniacs* comforter, worn from age and no longer zany to the max, was apathetically draped across the bed in his small bedroom that doubled as an office. He had been shuttered in trying to write. He had tried writing in his living room/kitchenette, but always found a distraction or some excuse not to sit in front of his old, white laptop. He would spot a drip where he had spilled his coffee earlier, or a single crystal of amber-colored raw sugar from said coffee, on his faux granite countertop, and be compelled to take a rag to it. Or, he'd get caught up in his bathroom/closet (he had a habit of hanging up his button-down shirts on the shower curtain tension rod to dry to save money on the complex's coin-op dryer), sitting on the toilet well after he had finished, reading a dog-eared Calvin and Hobbes anthology. Or, the refrigerator's whir would begin to sound like a refrigerator-whir rendition of "Hollaback Girl" and he would surrender, giving up all hope for productivity.

Writing had been hard as of late for Charlie, but he guessed it always had been a tough slog. He hoarded notebooks in high school, wishing he had something to fill their pages. He'd buy a new black-and-white composition book, or a nice journal, or a pack of five pocket-sized notebooks, and then do nothing with them except stare at them and feel guilty. There was that brief period though, a couple of summers ago, when he had written in a mad dash, completing a full-length feature screenplay in mere days. But he had been inspired then, for what felt like the first time.

His phone alarm buzzed, and the screen read: *Go to work or call to quit*. Charlie weighed the options, sighed again, and reached for his khakis and his dark blue polo shirt with the Popcorn Movies logo on the breast—a deranged, bug-eyed bucket of popcorn with a mad grin, inexplicably grasping a smaller, non-anthropomorphic bucket of popcorn in hand. The shirt was size *L*, for the *Large* amount of shame he felt while wearing it. Popcorn Movies was a large movie rental chain most well known for their ridiculous, yet somehow popular, one hundred rentals for $100 promotion. Charlie had worked there for a couple of years and hated it. But he lied to himself that at least he could watch all the movies he wanted, which would be good research for his future filmmaking career. After all, Quentin Tarantino worked in a movie rental spot, and so had Adam Brody.

He needed to save money for his eventual journey west. He had roughly calculated what it would cost to live for a couple of months in Los Angeles while he got on his feet. He was nowhere close to his savings goal, only pulling enough hours to pay his monthly bills and buy a couple of bottles of cheap red wine on the weekends. The number he had set for himself to save was etched in his mind as a not-so-friendly reminder of his inadequacy. He guessed he could move back in with his parents, but he'd rather wear a T-shirt that said *I GIVE UP* and a hat that said *LOOK DOWN AT MY SHIRT*.

Charlie pulled into the Popcorn Movies parking lot in his hand-me-down Isuzu. He looked up at the store's marquee. The *O*, *P*, and *C* of the backlit sign were out, making the sign proclaim, simply, *PORN MOVIES*. His hand moved towards the ignition to turn the car off but stopped before his fingers hit the keychain. Instead, he popped that sonofagun into drive and mashed the gas pedal with both feet. He drove straight into the mostly glass front of the store with a satisfying crash.

Just kidding—wishful thinking. In real life, he turned off the car and trudged into the store like a good little worker bee.

• • •

Roheed Mahaad had grown as much facial hair as he could, which wasn't a ton, to hide his babyish face. He was in his late teens, but looked years younger. He had grown a couple of inches in the past handful of years and his chest had broadened, but the softness in his eyes remained. He had cut the shaggy black hair that aged him down even younger and replaced the former curls with a hip new cut. He stood in the boardroom of a sunny glass office building in the Bay Area. He was in the heart of the tech world, near the city whose name could not be shortened without sounding insufferable—San Fran, Frisco, Sandy Franny. Usually, the kind of room he was in would have a long wooden table with fancy leather chairs, and the men who sat in said chairs would be stuffy white fifty-somethings in expensive but ill-fitting suits. However, this boardroom was inhabited by cool, multiracial, and non-gender-specific twenty-somethings in cardigans and hoodies and beat-up New Balances and fresh Nikes and moderately broken in Sauconys, chillaxin' on bean bag chairs or behind rolling standing desks.

Roheed was pitching an app to the room. He held up his smartphone, and as he used his finger to scroll and swipe through the various menus and features of the application, a projector displayed his actions on a screen behind him in real time.

"With this app, you can find someone who has a skill or service that you need, and in turn, you provide something they need. This provides an equal, almost symbiotic relationship with the person," Roheed said. There were slight nods of understanding from the room. A barefoot dude with prematurely grey hair made a finger tent in front of his mouth and furrowed his brow.

Roheed continued, "So, say, oh, for example someone needs to learn how to swim to compete in the Tri-County Relay Race to impress the girl of their dreams, and another person secretly lives in the guard house of a community swim and racquet club and needs their secret to be kept but knows how to teach swimming lessons." The creatives in the room were beginning to smell what Roheed was cooking.

"One person learns to swim and one person continues to live in secret. They both win!"

The head nerd of the company smiled. "That's an oddly specific example."

Roheed shrugged. "Or you could use it if you needed a cup of flour and someone else needed a unicycle, whatever."

"What do you call the app?" a guy with a man-bun and high-waters asked from the back of the room.

"I call it . . ." Roheed smiled. "'High Dive.'"

A stylized image of the Yellow County Community Swim and Racquet Club's original high diving board came up on the projection with a savvy High Dive logo emblazoned on it. The room clapped. The head nerd walked from behind his standing desk, shook Roheed's hand, and pulled Roheed in for a bro hug.

• • •

After another soul-sucking shift of standing behind an outdated computer cash register system, checking out movies for old people, high people, and high old people, Charlie drove home in his '90s-era car that his mom, the lovely Hilda Heralds, finally let him buy from her. He arrived at his apartment and hung his messenger bag on the coat rack by its strap, right next to an old trench coat with the dress shirt collar and cuffs sewn onto it.

His mail was on the floor after being dropped through the slot earlier that day by the mailperson. Charlie didn't quite understand why the mail slot was a thing; there was a different, better invention—the mailbox. It seemed pretty stupid and a little bit sad to Charlie that his mail just had to free-fall from a simple hole cut in a door to lie in wait on the floor until one returned home, opened the door, and treaded over the waiting mail, potentially ripping or crumpling an envelope or disturbing a packet of coupons. But there were bigger fish to fry, Charlie supposed, and that reminded him that he was hungry and he had a big fish thawing in the refrigerator.

He headed towards the kitchen, stepping with care over

his bills and credit card offers, when a particular piece of mail piqued his peepers.

• • •

Across the nation, after being ushered by the head nerd through the ultra-modern tech office where he had just presented, and Segwaying through the lush quad crawling with hipster geeks to his rented electric, self-driving, and self-parking smart car, Roheed arrived back at the house where he was renting a room.

The house was huge and a revolving door of app developers and start-up hopefuls and coders and the like rented rooms there month-to-month. Some went back to their hometowns to become addicted to video games and energy drinks after their perceived failure in the tech town; some moved on to buy even bigger houses than the one where Roheed was staying.

A cute, nerdy girl whose thumbs poked out of the cuffs of her American Apparel sweatshirt walked by sipping coffee and looking at her phone. Roheed smiled at her as a hello, but she didn't notice.

"You've got mail," she said, not looking up from her phone or even stuttering in her swift steps. Roheed checked his phone, confused. "You mean like old school mail?

"Yes, hashtag snail mail," she said. Roheed was intrigued.

Roheed and Charlie discovered the contents of the light blue, hand-addressed envelope at the same time, three thousand miles apart. The envelope said "Poole" in the upper left-hand corner, with a Yellow County address underneath. They each opened the envelope to discover a wedding invitation to Jonathan Poole and Chris "The Diving Broad" Partee's wedding.

Roheed was elated. He grinned broadly, already making a mental checklist of things to do to prepare for the sojourn back to Yellow County for the nuptials of his good friends. His mind was giddy as he thought, *I'm going back to Yellow County!*

Charlie was less enthused. He tried to think of excuses as to why he wouldn't be able to go to an in-town wedding for a friend who he looked up to in a weird way, a guy who he had worked with during a very pivotal summer of his life. Jonathan had really done him a solid by posing as his internship mentor to his dad. But Charlie wanted to spare himself the embarrassment of having to explain to the other guests why he hadn't made it out of Yellow County. *I can't believe I'm still in Yellow County,* Charlie thought as he removed that big fish from his refrigerator for dinner.

CHAPTER 2

WATER SPLASHED FROM the churning pool onto the medium grey tiled floor. The lanes were a flurry of arms and legs as swimmers butterfly-stroked furiously. Cheers echoed off the slightly tinted windows that made up the walls of the Yellow County Community College Indoor Pool and Fitness Facility.

College kids waved YCCC flags as they sat in the bleachers as Jonathan Poole paced the length of the pool. He was striking, with breathtaking blue eyes and usually wild chestnut-colored hair tamed and just a bit of salt creeping into his sideburns. He was wearing his YCCCIPFF windbreaker, size *L* for the *Large* amount of respect that he received while wearing it and even without it on, but it was a little loose because he was fit as a fab fiddle, and he didn't eat Fiddle Faddle.

He clapped his hands, yelling encouragement to the young YCCC student-athletes in the pool swimming their hearts out.

"Let's go, Yellow!" he praised.

On the other side of the indoor pool, in the visitors section, sat the fans of the other college's swim team. The Brown State swim team was a motley crew. The twins, brother Channan and sister Shannon Twinsley, were there of course, sitting very close, sharing a large brown towel with the school's insignia. They were usually described as "creepily close" and shared beautiful yet somewhat outdated Michael Pitt from *Funny Games* hair styles. Then there were a couple of other chuckleheads and chuckleheadettes, but the one who stood out the most was a young man in his early twenties named Scott.

Scott, the captain of the Brown State Swim Team, had a swimmer's body and a prisoner's face. His left eye was severely disfigured and the scar tissue pulled his right eye towards the center of his face. His eyes were so close together that from a distance it looked like he had just one. In fact, he was nearly blind in the disfigured eye, compounding his cyclopean appearance. He was squinting menacingly at the water and sneering as his teammates fell behind.

With the sound of the whistle, the heat was over. Yellow County Community got the first and second ribbons, among others. Jonathan clapped the winning swimmers on their backs and led them into a friendly huddle, while Scott also pulled his fellow swimmers aside, barking incoherent insults at them. Jonathan's swimmers smiled and congratulated one another, while Scott's team shriveled like beaten dogs.

Charlie wandered into the indoor pool area, hands stuffed deep into his pockets, and took a seat in the Yellow County section. He made eye contact with Jonathan, who gave him a big smile and a friendly nod. Charlie self-consciously nodded back, looking around to see if anyone saw the exchange. He let his eyes wander like Emile Hirsch in that movie where he wandered a bunch, until his gaze rested upon a beautiful young lady in the Brown State bleachers.

Charlie's eyes focused on only her, the rest of the indoor pool and fitness facility blurring around her. She had a clipboard in hand and she was taking down the last heat's ranking order. *She must be the Brown State swim team manager*, Charlie thought. Her hair looked so soft and her Brown State T-shirt, size *S* for the *Small* amount that it left to the imagination, fit her just so. She looked up.

Oh no! Charlie thought.

It was Jill Bateman.

• • •

Charlie flashed back to the snack bar of the Yellow County Community Swim and Racquet Club on a particularly memorable

Memorial Day weekend. Jill Bateman, then a fourteen-year-old (and three quarters!) first-year snack bar employee, struggled with her hollow-boned bird arms to open an industrial-sized tub of ranch-style salad dressing. Her YCCSRC T-shirt was knotted on the side to expose a little bit of midriff, size *XS* for *Xtra Sexiness*. She hadn't quite figured out what to do with her hair yet and was all limbs and no torso, but that wasn't slowing her down.

An eighteen-year-old Charlie chatted with Roheed, then in his mid-teens, as they did the dishes on that opening day of the pool's fiftieth season. They were talking about Charlie recently graduating high school and the emptiness he felt, but he kept a careful eye on Jill to make sure she didn't make a mess. Sure enough, when she got the ranch open, she spilled it all over the floor.

Charlie said, "Hold that thought," to Roheed, grabbed some rags, and handed them to Jill. She began sopping up the creamy dressing. Charlie returned to the sink and looked over at Jill who was bending to clean up the spilled goop and looking back over her shoulder enticingly. She put her finger in the white puddle and licked it. Charlie was grossed out.

Jill was nice enough, but she was a kid, and that whole summer after that she had made it very apparent that she wanted to get down and dirty—whatever she had thought that meant at the time—with Charlie boy. Not that Charlie was great with girl stuff, but he was most certainly not going to have a summer fling with a tween.

• • •

Charlie snapped back to the present and gasped.

Jill was now grown up—and hot! She looked up from her clipboard and made eye contact with Charlie from across the pool. He whipped his eyes away from hers, pretending that he didn't see her. He pretended to check his phone, he pretended that he was listening to a song by The Pretenders, he pretended that he had just remembered that he needed to go preheat some tenders. He pretended that his phone was all of a sudden alerting him that he must go outside absolutely that instant. He hightailed it right on out of that indoor pool and fitness facility.

Charlie speed-walked across the quad, escaping the situation. He crossed the lush lawn where coeds were sunbathing, throwing the 'bee, and even hackying a sack or two.

A voice called out to him, "Charlie? Charlie Heralds?" He couldn't not turn around, so he didn't not.

Jill strolled up to him, almost in slow motion. If this was some cheesy movie, it most definitely would have been in slow motion, with lens flares, and Jill would have tossed her hair to some song that would be hot during post-production, but totes outdated by the time the flick hit theaters and same day video on demand. But this wasn't a movie, so Jill walked up at an average speed with no embellished lighting or soundtrack of any kind. Even in the natural light with ambient sound, Charlie still felt uneasy and off-balance. He hadn't seen Jill since that last day of summer—several years ago, he guessed.

"Hey, Charlie." Jill's voice was more mature than before but still feminine. It melted into Charlie's eardrums like java lava.

Charlie played the fool. "Mhm?"

"It's me, Jill."

"Jill, Jill, Jill . . . hmm." Charlie thought he was slick.

Jill could see through Charlie's nonchalant ruse like an x-ray of Swiss cheese. "Oh shut up, Charlie. You remember me, Jill Bateman. We worked together in the snack bar at the Yellow County Community Swim and Racquet Club the summer before last."

Charlie paused. "That couldn't have been just two summers ago."

"Oh, you're right, because I was fourteen and three quarters at the time." Jill smiled. "And now I'm eighteen."

The word "eighteen" echoed through the whole quad, or maybe just in Charlie's mind. His jaw dropped, he tried to compose himself.

"What are you doing here?" he asked, but realized that it sounded like an indictment more than a wonderment. "I mean, I thought you were going to go here," he gestured to the YCCC in general, "but I haven't seen you around."

Jill gestured to her T-shirt, giving Charlie an excuse to break eye contact and look at her chest. "I go to Brown State. I'm the swim team manager."

"Buck Frown State," Charlie said mainly to himself, force of habit.

"What?"

"They're our rivals."

"Our?"

Charlie gestured again to the community college they inhabited. "I take a couple classes here when I'm not working."

Jill's pocket chimed and she checked her phone. "The next heat is about to start. I gotta get in there. But it was great running into you. I'm glad we could *meet*." She raised an eyebrow and tilted her head toward the swim complex. "Get it? Meet?"

"Cute." Charlie said.

She turned to go but looked back as she walked away. "Maybe we can run into each other on purpose next time."

Charlie's feet were cemented to the sidewalk, his throat felt like sandpaper's itchy uncle. "That would be awesome," he croaked.

She walked away.

He watched.

Roheed walked up behind Charlie and put his hand on Charlie's shoulder. Charlie jumped a little. He was expecting Roheed to arrive at some point—Roheed would be staying with him for the weekend—but he didn't expect him in that moment, while he was still in the Jill afterglow.

"Is that . . . ?" Roheed began.

"Jill Bateman," Charlie finished.

"She turned into quite an attractive young lady."

Charlie just nodded.

"That must be very confusing to you."

Charlie nodded again as they watched Jill sashay back into the YCCCIPFF.

CHAPTER 3

BACK AT THE indoor pool, Charlie and Roheed sat in the Yellow County cheering section. Roheed was enthralled with the proceedings, whooping it up for his home county of Yellow, while Charlie couldn't keep his mind off Jill, trying his best to keep his peepers from peeping in her direction so as not to make eye contact with her again. Roheed was right to be caught up. Charlie was right too because Jill was now a super-hot, legal young lady.

It was the last heat. Matt Hedge, fully recovered from the hernia he sustained from sneezing while pooping and the subsequent surgery, and several more YCCC swimmers were lined up on their marks, as well as Scott, the Twinsley twins, and a couple of other Brown State swimmers.

Scott lowered his custom uni-goggle over his one functioning eye. Matt, Shannon and Channan, and the rest bent at the waist, poising their bodies to dive in and hit the water, hoping for an early lead. The whistle blew and the race was on like The King of Kong. The swimmers blazed back and forth, Matt and Scott neck and neck ahead of the rest of the pack. Scott craned his neck to locate Matt. He let out an angry burst of bubbles from his mouth when he saw they were tied. Matt's muscled arms, one of them baring the generic tribal sun he had gotten well before his eighteenth birthday at the Red Octopus, dove in and out of the water, propelling him forward. On their last lap, Scott edged ahead by a single kick but Matt regained his ground. Their hands hit the side of the pool at the same second, and a whistle toot signified the end of the whole, as William Hung would say, shebang.

The officials conferred for just a tad, probably not long enough, until one of them walked over and handed the first-place ribbon to Matt Hedge. Scott couldn't believe it; he about jumped out of his skin. He gave an unaware Matt the evil eye—he only had one, but it was evil as hell, and he knew how to give it. His view panned over to Jonathan yakking it up with the Yellow County team. Scott's rage redirected to Jonathan. He shook his head as he stared at Jonathan, angry at his happiness. Scott used his index finger to point to his good eye, and then he pointed it at Jonathan. He took his thumb and drew it across his throat, and that's almost never a good sign!

A little while later, at dusk, as the crowd dispersed from the event, Jonathan exited the Yellow County Community College Indoor Pool and Fitness Facility with Roheed and Charlie. They walked across the quad, heading towards Jonathan's office in a nearby administrative building. An angry voice called out to them.

"Hey!"

Jonathan turned. It was Scott, and he was pissed.

"That race was a *tie*!" Scott clopped over to them. He was wearing a Brown State Swim tracksuit and Chain Male sandal slides over crisp white socks.

Roheed and Charlie were confused. "Which race?" Charlie said.

"Me and that clown Matt, we tied. Brown State would have won if it weren't for that bull hockey call. You had the officials in your pocket like a dirty snot rag."

Jonathan was about to pull his dirty snot rag out of his pocket to wipe his anger-moistened brow but realized that would only help Scott's argument. "Sounds like your loser bone is a little sore," Jonathan said. "Don't worry, put a little ice on it, take two 'I don't give a cares,' and *don't* call me in the morning."

That quip just riled Scott up all the more. "You think you're really funny," he said through gritted teeth.

Roheed, not knowing his role, piped up, "I actually thought that was pretty humorous."

Scott looked at Roheed with a look that would make a dandelion die. "You know what won't be funny?"

"Anything that hack Jerd McKinley craps out?" Charlie asked, not really in the conversation.

"No," Scott said, confused but then ready to be angry again.

"Every human being on the planet's certain and eventual death?" Jonathan ventured.

"Let me just tell you what won't be funny," Scott was done with letting these obvious jokesters give their jokety-joke answers to his, in his opinion, very serious question. "It won't be funny when I get you back for cheating to win this meet. I don't know when or how, but it's going to suck for you. And I'll be just laughing and laughing." He let out a laugh that sounded like a duck choking on a chicken wing.

"I thought you said it wasn't going to be funny," Charlie said with a smirk.

Scott steamed. "You are so lucky that I have to ride home with my brother and sister or I would be stabbing you right now." And he stormed off in a huff, leaving Jonathan, Charlie, and Roheed feeling like they had dodged a one-eyed bullet, but also with an impending sense of dread because who knew what a guy like that could be capable of.

The dread quickly passed and was forgotten when they arrived at Jonathan's office and began catching up in earnest. Jonathan handed a beer to Charlie but when he offered one to Roheed he politely declined and asked instead for a tea or a sparkling water, perhaps. He was not yet of age and had never drank an alcoholic beverage before.

While Jonathan heated up some water to prepare a yerba mate for Roheed from his emergency mate stash, Roheed perused the brochure for the Yellow County Community College Chapel.

"That's our venue," Jonathan said, referring to the chapel the brochure was describing.

The chapel itself was cute, the brochure poorly made, highlighting the inadequacies of the location. Blurbs proclaimed "Nearly asbestos free" and "Come smell our pews!" In one of the photos of a decorative mirror, you could see the photographer and he was wearing Crocs. Roheed thought it was a bit silly that the ornate windows were referred to as "purposefully stained"—they should have just said "beautiful stained glass windows"—but brochure-making wasn't his game, so he guessed he'd let it go. He was happy for Jonathan and excited to be back in town for the affair.

"Exquisite venue," he said to Jonathan, who smiled and handed him a hot gourd of yerba mate, "and thanks for the mate."

Jonathan smiled, "Yerba mate is myba yerte, my friend."

Swim team trophies and plaques lined the walls and the shelves, most from the Yellow County Community Swim and Racquet Club swim team, and some from his new gig at the college. A photo of Jonathan and "Wild" Bill Peterson, Jonathan's mentor until he died tragically, sat on a frame on the large desk in the corner. A CPR dummy (Tim) dressed in YCCC garb stood proudly in the corner of the room. There was a cot set up as well.

Roheed gestured to the cot. "Are you secretly living *here* now?" referring to a couple of summers before when Jonathan was caught living in the guard house of the YCCSRC when he was the head lifeguard.

• • •

Jonathan remembered the particular summer that Roheed was referring to and the previous summers when he had lived in the small room with the timecard clock and the safe and the calendar on the wall and the CPR dummy (Tim) and everything else needed for a fully functioning lifeguard office. He had slept on the cot meant for sun-stroked seniors and bee-stung boys and girls. He would get up early before the pool opened and shower in the men's locker room, wearing his faded red lifeguard shorts and whistle dangling from a lanyard.

The shower was an open area with four communal showerheads, and sometimes, if he felt like treating himself, he would turn on all four, point them to the center of the tiled room, and let the steaming water cascade down his body over his generous chest hair. He would pull his shorts away from his body with his thumb and drip soapy, sudsy water down into his nether region.

In the snack bar he would make himself breakfast as he licked a red-white-and-blue Rocket Pop or a purple Fla-Vor-Ice or even sometimes a Sonic the Hedgehog Popsicle with gumball eyes. He always wore his favorite apron, the one that said, *Kiss the Cook . . . Please!!!?!* Then he would eat his breakfast at one of the picnic tables in the outdoor dining area as he looked out over the pool.

On the surface, he had enjoyed those summers, the seasons in the between not so much. It was very lonely living in the closed club. He had known deep down that the lifestyle could not last. It took finding a love like Chris, and being kicked out of course, to wrest him from his womblike haven. He knew he would always feel bittersweet, even nostalgic, when he looked back at that time, like one might romanticize a high school relationship that in reality hadn't ended well. Hindsight had a way of clearing things up, but that same time playing tricks on your memory, rose-coloring what, at the time, was actually pretty sucky.

• • •

Charlie brought Jonathan back from his thoughts. "Yeah, are you going to get fired again?" Charlie asked.

"I'm just staying here until the wedding," Jonathan replied. "After we got engaged, Chris and I thought it would be romantic to live apart for a while. That way the wedding night would be extra spicy." He wiggled his eyebrows up and down in a way that Charlie found very unsettling. Charlie shuddered. "The Dean knows the plan," Jonathan continued. "She's cool with it. She said it was romantic."

"Good," Roheed said, he and Charlie trying their darndest to keep from picturing Jonathan and his bride-to-be in any sort of sexual scenario.

"I'm really glad you guys are here for the wedding by the way," Jonathan said.

"Wouldn't miss it for the world," Roheed said genuinely.

"I just live super close to here, so it wasn't an issue," Charlie began. Jonathan shot him a look and he finished with, "But I'm excited, too!"

• • •

Chris "The Diving Broad" Partee had sauntered into Jonathan's life when she came to the pool to sell them a new high dive after their former diving board had come unlashed in a freak storm and landed on the patriarch of the pool, "Wild" Bill Peterson, killing him instantly. Chris was unique, masculine in a feminine way. She was outspoken and seemed like a good yang to Jonathan's yin.

She had worn her company polo a little tight in the sleeves to show off her size *L* guns. The back of the shirt had read, *The Diving Broad: More Splash, Less Cash*. At first, Jonathan thought the word *Broad* was a typo for *Board* and wondered why she would still wear a misprinted article of clothing. She was chewing tobacco and she was a little sweaty and her gruff confidence had attracted Jonathan instantly, even though it confused him.

If their relationship were to be judged solely on their first date, then you would have thought they didn't stand a chance. Jonathan didn't drive, so he opted to meet Chris downtown so he could take the metro. He didn't know many spots, so he took her to Ben's, a place he knew thanks to Charlie. He and Charlie had pulled off a semi-successful caper on Charlie's dad there once, when Charlie needed Jonathan to pretend he was Charlie's mentor at some internship he never really got the details about.

Chris was a meat-and-potatoes kind of gal who didn't expect to be wined and dined at a chili-dog joint. Jonathan had left his wallet in his other lifeguard shorts and she ended up paying. All that, and a misunderstanding when Jonathan asked her if she wanted to "blow his whistle," referring to the whistle he kept on a red lanyard on his person at all times, added up to a pretty disastrous date. Jonathan thought for sure he had blown it—the date, not the whistle—but his honesty and candor and unselfconscious humor delighted Chris. Just as Jonathan was intrigued by and drawn to her, so was she to him.

• • •

Charlie was excited that his friend had found love. *Good for him; at least someone had something going on in their lives,* Charlie thought. *Jonathan is getting married, and Roheed seems to be on the verge of some success . . .* He was the only one back in the rut where he seemed to fall every so often.

"You're looking well, Jonathan," Roheed said.

"I've lost some weight. I swore off all food that can be prepared in a snack bar so I can look my best for the wedding."

Charlie nodded. *Rock 'n roll, good for him.*

Jonathan pointed to Roheed. "What are you up to Mr. Fancy? Mr. California?"

Roheed smiled brightly. "I just sold my app! It's going to launch in the summer."

"That's awesome, congratulations!" Jonathan gushed. "How's Florence?"

Roheed's smile darkened a couple of shades. He had met Florence Comfortinn, the socialite heiress to the Comfort Inn fortune, the same summer that everything had happened with Bill dying and the Tri-County Relay Race. It had taken nearly all summer for Florence to cotton to Roheed, but they had been dating ever since, and they were happy*ish*.

"She's great," Roheed said. "You know, her reality web series really exploded and that opened up a lot of doors for her. She's been deejaying around Europe for a few months now. It's just tough having a long-distance relationship."

Charlie nodded, as if he knew. Roheed redirected the conversation towards him, "What is going on with you, Charlie? You never respond to my messages."

Charlie sipped his beer. "Yeah. I've just been busy I guess. I take classes here at Yellow County Community and I work at . . . um . . . Popcorn Movies."

"That's cool."

Charlie looked up. "It's not, but thanks for saying that."

"How's the writing going?" Roheed continued, not picking up on the obvious social cues that Charlie was telegraphing that he absolutely did not want to talk about himself. "Whatever happened to *In Sheep's Clothing*?"

Jonathan's eyes darted to Charlie who looked at his shoes.

"You wrote that and had the table read. I thought some people might get interested."

Charlie was bummed. "Yeah . . ."

Jonathan covered. "That sort of went away, right? But your next thing will be even bigger and better!"

Roheed narrowed his eyes and tilted his head.

"I'm saving up to move to LA though," Charlie blustered, "so that will happen at some point."

"Louisiana?" Jonathan asked.

"Los Angeles," Charlie replied, wanting to jump out of his skin and take his skeleton for a spin.

Jonathan nodded.

"Do you have a time frame on that?" Roheed asked, still not getting it.

Charlie said "No" with finality, tipped his can towards the heavens, and took a healthy guzzle.

The room got too quiet. Up above in the rafters a couple of crickets looked at each other like *this is awkward* and started chirping to fill the silent void.

Charlie broke the conversational stalemate. "Can you pass me another beer?" He crushed his can and tossed it aside. Jonathan handed him a fresh one. Charlie sipped it and smiled, the cold liquid warming his body from the inside.

"Hey, remember a few summers ago, when we all worked at the swim and racquet club?"

"Totally," Jonathan said.

"And like, June Summers was busting our beach balls and Roheed, you were just meeting Florence."

Roheed smiled.

"And Judas, freaking Judas," Charlie continued, "That traitor!"

"That was a *total* surprise," Jonathan was grinning too. "I did NOT see that coming."

"Right?" Charlie agreed.

And the gang fell back into their groove, reminiscing and laughing about the happenstances at the Yellow County Community Swim and Racquet Club a few summers before.

What they didn't see was Scott crouched in the hallway outside the office, just under the little window in the door, listening . . . waiting . . . and plotting.

CHAPTER 4

ROHEED WAS STAYING at Charlie's place. When he had left Yellow County a couple of years prior, his parents had immediately gutted his bedroom and put in a ping pong table and a mini-fridge. He didn't want to say anything, but he thought Charlie's apartment kind of sucked. There was a small bedroom that pretty much only fit Charlie's bed and laptop, a bizarre bathroom/closet arrangement, and a kitchen/dining room/living room combo with a couch and a small table for meals for one and it all seemed lonely to Roheed.

But Roheed was lonely as well. He waited up for a couple of hours that night for Florence to FaceTime or call or at least @ him on Instagram, but no @s came and he was left feeling like an @-hole. She did post several shots from her deejay booth of a roaring crowd in some foreign city, but no mention of the boy she left back in the States to wait while she toured the globe. He scrolled through her old pics, reminiscing of the times when they were together often. There was the picture of him and her eating crabs at the staff dinner at the swim and racquet club, one of Roheed at the Natural History Museum pretending to high-five a caveman, the very next picture of Florence pretending to be a raptor, and of course the photos from their road trip to Florence, Alabama, to visit the very Comfort Inn that Florence was named after.

Roheed's longing to be with her ached like an over-extended muscle. When he eventually fell asleep, with the social media app still open and resting on his face, his nose continually hearted and un-hearted a particular picture of she and him back at the YCCSRC a couple of summers ago after the big Tri-County Relay Race. They were both smiling, despite the outcome of the race.

• • •

The next day was to be dedicated to wedding-related events. Charlie and Roheed weren't sure exactly what they were in for; this was Jonathan they were talking about. But they waited outside of Charlie's apartment complex cautiously optimistic. A Hummer H2 stretch limo with a hot tub in the back rolled up. The window slowly *skritch*ed down, revealing Jonathan sitting in the back with his betrothed, Chris Partee, wearing her signature Diving Broad polo shirt, her hair slicked back, looking tough as nails but feminine as hell. Jonathan was grinning ear-to-ear. Chris, usually as cool as an unpickled pickle, was playing it cucumber, but Charlie could tell she was excited about the whole getting married ordeal. Of course, "Hollaback Girl" was thumping from the limo speakers.

Charlie gestured to the garish limousine. "What is this?"

"IYOGMO, bros," Jonathan said, obviously instigating.

"Eye ogg moe?" Roheed questioned.

Jonathan explained, "'Ideally, You Only Get Married Once,' you know, like YOLO!"

Charlie buried his face in his hand.

Roheed said, "Not the catchiest of phrases, but okay."

Jonathan was tired of trying to be cute. "Just get in."

Jonathan had brought his buddies from the swim and racquet club and Chris had brought her acquaintances from the diving board retail biz: Pat from Totally Board, Sydney from At The Dive In, and Alex from Thornblatt's Diving Boards and Diving Board Accessories.

Charlie popped the bottle of champagne that the limo had provided and sprayed it like they had just won the Tri-County Relay Race, to the annoyance of Chris's friends. Roheed modestly shook up a can of generic store-brand lemon-lime soda and let the bubbles escape without spraying innocent bystanders. One of Chris's buds had smuggled aboard a bottle of Jägermeister, but no one wanted to share in the experience of drinking a shot of licorice-tinged death liquid. Despite the fanfare with which Chris's friend had presented the liquor, she quietly sipped it once or twice and put it away.

At some point, after a few laps through the streets of Tuxedo, a nearby town with a strange name, and some donuts in the YCCSRC parking lot, they decided to hit the hot tub in the back of the stretched H2. They waved to passing traffic and splashed water on unlucky pedestrians that had lost the lottery of life and happened to be pedestry-ing at that very moment. Roheed pretended for just a sec that he couldn't swim and Jonathan sprang into action, his lifeguard reflexes taking hold. But then he remembered that Roheed could indeed swim, Roheed popped back up to the surface with a grin, and Jonathan conceded that he had been X'd like a punk. Charlie lifted his thin, pale leg out of the water and twiddled his Kevin Costner in *Waterworld*-esque webbed toes and everyone was thoroughly skeeved.

After a brief stint where for some reason Roheed was driving the limo and the driver hopped in the back to party with the crew, they hit a couple of spots in a Bladensburg strip mall (by the Village Thriftstore and the Checkers) for official wedding business. At the bakery, Jonathan and Chris tasted cake and icing combinations. Charlie and Roheed intertwined arms and fed each other cake just the same. In the jewelry store, where Jonathan and Chris were picking up their rings, Roheed iced himself out in garish chains and a Paul Wall-worthy grill. And at the flower shop, somehow Charlie convinced Roheed to strip and lay covered in rose petals, *American Beauty*-style, for Jonathan and Chris to find. A plastic bag floated by and Charlie filmed it with his phone with a dead-eyed stare in another take from the movie. Although Charlie and Roheed thought their shenanigans were hilarious, Chris's friends were perturbed. Jonathan wished he could get in on the fun but abstained in solidarity with Chris's crew, who all seemed to have excuses to leave the festivities early anyway.

The gang, minus Chris's guests, returned to the limo and headed back to Tuxedo to go to the local tuxedo store, Tuxedo Tuxedos. Jonathan burst from the changing room totally decked out in an all-white tux, the red lanyard and whistle fashioned into a bolo tie around his collar. He looked good. Chris emerged from another changing room in a black tux, the pants three-quarter-length and the dress shirt underneath the jacket a little frilly. She looked super punk rock.

"You look good, babe," Jonathan told her.

"You always do," she replied, and they kissed.

While still locked in their embrace, Chris looked deeply into Jonathan's eyes to the point where he knew something was wrong or at least weird.

"What are you doing?" he asked. "Why are you looking at me like that?"

"I want our wedding to be special," Chris began.

"It already is. It will be. What's going on?" Jonathan began looking around the haberdashery.

"And I think this is for the best," she continued.

"What's happening?"

An older woman, short, vibing with nervous energy, entered the store. She looked around until her peepers fell on Jonathan. Jonathan saw her but couldn't place her at first, his brain doing a Terminator-like scan of names and faces from his past to try and recognize this familiar lady. Who was she, with her salt-and-pepper hair, medium build, and piercing blue eyes?

Then it hit him.

"Mom?"

CHAPTER 5

WHEN JONATHAN'S DAD died in a freak accident (it seemed like his father and all his father figures happened to die in freak accidents) involving an industrial laundry press machine nicknamed The Mangler, Jonathan became the man of the house as a teen—for about a week, until his mom hooked up with his deceased dad's former co-worker Rick Sandlehanger. Rick had popped by to pay his respects and see if Jonathan's mom wanted to maybe share his twelve-pack of beer. On Jonathan's eighteenth birthday, Jonathan moved out of the house as Rick moved in. Having nowhere else to go, Jonathan camped out in the Yellow County Community Swim and Racquet Club guard office. He had set his box of belongings in the corner, thinking it was going to be a temporary solution, but days turned into weeks, weeks turned into months, and months turned into beautiful butterflies . . . or wait, *years*—sorry, not butterflies, years.

Jonathan hadn't seen his mother since, and he was nearly double those eighteen years now. Once or twice a summer she would stop by the YCCSRC to check on her estranged son, but Jonathan would see her coming and hide in the back of the snack bar by the large double freezer that held the paper bags of frozen French fries and the big tubs of ice cream for Ice Cream Night, or in one of the stalls in the bathroom, red lifeguard shorts pulled down around his ankles even though no business was being done due north. Every year, Jonathan would coach up a member of his staff what to do if his mom showed up. He'd tell him or her to explain to his mother that he no longer worked there, that he was an architect over in Annapolis, that everything was going great for him. But she knew that he was ducking her, and he knew that she knew, but they continued their charade, butterfly after butterfly.

So, Jonathan was in shock when he saw his mother, Tamara "Tammy" Cooper-Poole-Sandlehanger, in that tuxedo shop in Tuxedo, Maryland. She looked older than he expected, and tired. She was nervous to be there, her hands clutching her purse like it might run away from her if she didn't keep hold of it. Her smile was genuine though, cautious, but truly happy to see her boy.

"It is so good to see you," she said.

Jonathan ignored her and turned to Chris. "How could you?" he said. Without waiting for a response or permission, Jonathan ran out of the tuxedo store, still wearing his white tux.

Chris called after him, "Jonathan!" but he was already gone.

The salesman who had been helping their party with their measurements and such approached Chris, Charlie, Roheed, and Tammy, a weary look on his mug.

"Uh . . ." he began, and gestured towards the space where Jonathan used to be standing. "So, is he going to rent that tux?"

• • •

Jonathan sat in the food court at a booth all his own. His table was piled high with the type of fare you find in a food court or snack bar: French fries, burgers, mozzarella stix, nachos with orangey goop masquerading as cheese, and of course, a damned chicken quesadilla. He was on a hardcore binge, trying to eat away the feelings of seeing his mother after so long.

Charlie approached him cautiously. "Can I sit?"

Jonathan bit into one of the burgers and ketchup dribbled onto the jacket of the white tux he was still wearing. Charlie shuddered; the fresh stain looked like a gunshot wound in a Tarantino movie.

"I don't care," Jonathan said, his mouth full of churning ground beef and bread and condiments.

Charlie was confused. "You don't care if I sit or you don't care that you just ketchup-popsicled your jacket?"

Jonathan's eyes just flamed and he went back to gorging. So, Charlie sat.

"Hey, so that was your mom, huh?"

No response from Jonathan, just chewing.

Charlie continued. "That's cool though, she came for your wedding. That's exciting."

Jonathan swallowed. He wiped his face on the sleeve of the— let me remind you, *white*—tuxedo jacket.

"Yeah," he said. "Yeah, super cool that the mother who abandoned me, right after my dad died, for a new man, randomly showed up in my life after years! Pretty, uh, 'cool.'"

"Well when you put it that way . . ." Charlie shrugged.

But Jonathan was on a roll. "And Chris didn't even tell me ahead of time, she just surprised me today, like I was a punk that Jamie Kennedy *X*'d, when we're supposed to be wrapping up wedding stuff. I thought we had no secrets."

"She just wants what's best for you."

Jonathan's usually bright eyes had a little less light behind them. "Maybe this wedding isn't what's best for me, then." He took an indiscriminate handful of nachos and stuffed it into his mouth. A hefty glurp of toxic orange cheese skydived onto his lapel. Then he stood and flipped the table as he walked off, leaving Charlie sitting in the midst of a huge mess.

Charlie called after him. "So I guess no more bachelor party tonight?"

Jonathan didn't turn around but paused to say, "No, the bachelor party is still on regardless." He started walking again and then said, more to himself than to Charlie, "I'm getting demolished tonight."

CHAPTER 6

LATER, AT CHARLIE'S apartment, Charlie and Roheed were in that state of undress in which they were basically ready but still had some buckles to buckle, buttons to button, and scraggly hairs on the backs of their heads to smooth.

Roheed sat on Charlie's couch, his back hitting the armrest and his legs not quite fitting on the short sofa. Charlie sat on the floor against the couch, a Mason jar three-quarters full with cheap red wine. He didn't know much about wine and he couldn't remember a lot from the movie *Sideways*, but he did recall Paul Giamatti freaking out about merlot, so he always bought the pinot noir on the bottom shelf. They were watching TV mindlessly, each in their own world, when a movie trailer began that caught their attention.

A voice-over artist with a deep, important voice began: "This summer . . ." Fade in to a drunk girl stumbling through a dark wood. A wolf appears from nowhere, running, snarling. A scream. Smash cut to black as the scream echoes.

The VO artist continued, "A *tail* about a girl who doesn't know *where* her life is headed." Fade in on a small, collegiate apartment. The girl from the woods has a huge bite wound on her leg. "Does this look infected to you?" she asks her roommate.

The roommate looks at the nasty gash and shrugs. "Nothing a little alcohol won't fix." She smiles. Jump cut to the roommate and the girl taking several shots of clear liquor in succession.

Roheed's eyes darted from the TV to Charlie and back. He was confused at Charlie's increasing agitation. Charlie pawed around for the remote, spilling his red wine on the carpet in the process. "Oh jeez Louise," he said, annoyed.

The trailer continued with a shot of a full moon, the audio of a wolf howling in the distance, and landed on the girl in a bathroom shaving her legs. She holds up her razor and sees thick, wiry black hair all over the blade. Extreme close up on her eyes widening in shock, then a whip zoom out to show her appalled face as she looks down and sees that she is transforming into a *werewolf!* She screams, and the screen cuts to black, her scream echoing.

"She just knows that life as a werewolf . . ." the VO artist continued, with a sly smile in his voice, "bites."

Picture up on the girl and her roommate as they stand in a studio with fashion pieces all around. "The fashion show is on the eighth," the roommate tells the girl.

"The eighth!" the girl gasps. "The eighth is the next full moon. I can't put on a career-launching fashion show . . ." whip zoom in to her face, "if I'm a werewolf!"

The VO continued over quick shots from the upcoming film in rapid succession: a werewolf tears through the collegiate apartment kitchen, a large fashion show is full of onlookers, models put on werewolf masks. "From Executive Producer Jerd McKinley . . ." said the VO artist.

The girl and a guy flirt in a college hallway, and the girl looks at the guy nervously. "I'm Leonora, Leonora Sheep."

She smiled as the VO artist revealed, finally, the title of the movie, "*In Sheep's Clothing,*" and the trailer ended.

Charlie dabbed up the red wine he had spilled with a paper towel and found the remote too late. Roheed stared at the television, mouth agape. Charlie switched off the TV and stormed out of the room.

Roheed called after him, "Charlie, Jerd stole your idea?"

Charlie called back, "I don't want to talk about it."

Roheed, still confused, repeated himself, only this time as a statement and not a question. "Jerd stole your idea." Charlie's only response was to slam his bedroom door shut.

Roheed guessed that he could Bing more information about the movie that Jerd had apparently stolen from Charlie. But he preferred to get the truth from the horse's mouth, Charlie being the horse in this scenario, and his mouth being the mouth. Now just wasn't the time, so instead he shrugged and scrolled through his phone to find his girlfriend, Florence Comfortinn, in his recent contacts list. He video-called her. After a few rings, the call connected, and her overly made-up face popped up on-screen.

"Hey babe!" Florence yelled over the music and crowd noise in what looked to Roheed like a packed dance club in his limited vista through the phone's screen.

"Hey, Florence," he said with a sad smile, missing her.

Florence nodded towards the crowd. "I'm just about to do a set."

"Oh, okay." Roheed felt deflated; he had hoped that he would catch her at a time where they could enjoy each other's e-company. There was a short window every so often when, despite the time zone difference and Florence's night-owlism and day sleep-titude, sometimes they were both awake and free and able to chat for a few minutes.

"I'm sorry we keep missing each other." Florence cute-frowned, then smiled.

"Yeah," Roheed ugly-smiled, then grimaced; his version of the facial expressions Florence had just exhibited were way less cute when he did them.

Florence looked past her phone and listened for a moment to something that Roheed couldn't decipher. She smiled and laughed at whatever Roheed couldn't see.

Roheed fake-smiled. "Who are you talking to?"

"Huh?" Florence pulled her attention back to the screen. "Oh, no one. No one."

A dude's face popped onto Florence's screen. He stuck out his tongue and waggled it back and forth. Florence laughed and pushed him off-screen. "You're such a Yakko," she said, presumably to the tongue-waggling dude just off-screen.

Roheed fumed. "Was that Alabaster Sixx?"

But Florence's connection started to suck. She froze, glitched out, and then the screen went blank.

"Hello? Hello? What?" Roheed tried to reconnect, but his phone informed him that Florence could not be reached. He was pissed.

"Charlie!" he yelled.

"What?" Charlie answered from the next room, annoyed.

"I would like an alcoholic beverage!"

Charlie popped his head into the room. "Really?"

"I feel that it is a necessity at this juncture," Roheed said calmly, even though his heart was racing. He had never had an alcoholic drink before, but he figured tonight was as good a time as any, you know, while he was frustrated and confused.

Charlie looked at the clock on the wall—it was five o'clock on the dot—and shrugged. "It's five o'clock somewhere," he said, and handed Roheed a light beer.

Roheed cracked it and took a sip. His eyes went wide. He took another sip, thinking the beer tasted like rubbing alcohol diluted with fermented apple juice and then farted on by a stale bagel. Then he thought the taste was actually growing on him and the lightheaded sensation he was already feeling was pleasant. At that moment, he decided that he was not going to let his potential issues with Florence harsh his mell' and that the upcoming night was going to be, as the kids were saying those days, *epic*.

Roheed and Charlie finished their version of getting ready for a night out. Charlie sort of pushed his hair the way that it wanted to go. Roheed tied his necktie in the mirror. Charlie shrugged on a coat. Roheed put his cuff links through his shirt cuffs. Charlie drank more bottom-shelf pinot noir and Roheed had another light beer, so Charlie was feeling nicely lubricated and Roheed was pretty lit. Jonathan pulled up outside of Charlie's apartment complex, sitting shotgun in a Hitch, which was like an Uber or a Lyft except the drivers also gave you bad dating advice while they drove you around. He reached over the Hitch driver's lap to honk the horn. Charlie and Roheed hopped in the car and they were off.

After suffering through Armando's poor driving and horrendous dating tips—"If she has a twin you get to choose" and "Of course you can respond to a text with an email"—Jonathan, Roheed, and Charlie rolled up to a club on the edge of Yellow County, near the Maryland–DC line, called Da Club, the very club 50 Cent was referring to in that song where he proclaimed that we could all "find (him) in Da Club." They looked quite a sight, walking three abreast, seemingly in slow motion like *Reservoir*

Dogs. Jonathan wore a flashy suit over his lifeguard polo, a size *M*, no longer very snug due the *Medium* amount of self-restraint he had shown in the months leading up to the wedding. Charlie didn't own a lot of dress clothes, so he was back in his trench coat costume that he had once worn to trick his parents into thinking that he had an internship in DC in order to clandestinely manage the YCCSRC snack bar for another summer. Roheed actually looked legitimately cool in a nice tailored suit, expensive sneakers, and a fitted hat, but he walked a little loosey-goosey due to the two beers he had ingested.

They reached the velvet rope of Da Club where a bouncer stood, nipples hard underneath a tight-fitting, black muscle shirt, size *L* for the *Large* amount of power he wielded over the small domain that was the door to that particular club. He didn't even refer to his clipboard, instead looking the trio up and down once before he said, "No."

The bravado with which they had approached the club fell away like the seeds of a dandelion. They turned to slink away.

A voice called to them, "Hey losers!"

They looked up to see none other than Judas Traditore, the bastard who had once betrayed their relay race team, standing in the doorway of Da Club, grinning like the pug that found the peanut butter.

CHAPTER 7

CHARLIE HADN'T SEEN Judas in years and yet there he was, dressed in long, pointy, expensive-looking dress shoes, tight, shiny slacks, and a Chain Male polo shirt. One sleeve mostly covered what had to be a huge brand on his shoulder of the Greek letter beta. He hadn't aged at all; in fact, if anything, he looked better, younger. His hair was finely pomaded and his cheeks, top and bottom, were chiseled from granite.

"Are you coming in the club or what?" he said in a curt but oddly friendly way. He put his arm around the beefy bouncer. "They're with me." He slipped the bouncer a ten spot and the bouncer begrudgingly unclipped the velvet rope, gesturing for Charlie, Roheed, and Jonathan to pass through.

The club was packed. Judas wound their group through the dudes with spiky hair who were fist-pumping to the music and the ladies in short dresses who were dancing and holding their phones in one hand and a poorly mixed cocktail with a thin black straw in the other. They reached Judas's table, where he had the mother of all bottle service setups spread out, bottle service unlike anything Charlie had ever seen. Judas had clear liquor in goblets, mixer juices in all the colors of the rainbow, limes and olives and other garnishes, and even a baby bottle, a stuffed bottle-nosed dolphin toy, and a Blu-ray copy of the movie *Bottle Rocket*. At Da Club, they don't skimp on the bottle service.

"Help yourself," Judas said as he gestured to the bevy of beverages.

Charlie, Jonathan, and Roheed attacked the drinks like lions on a weak gazelle. They each had their reasons for getting plastered that night. For Charlie, seeing the *In Sheep's Clothing* movie trailer had reopened a wound that he had tried to bury deep. Roheed was sad not only about his most recent conversation with Florence and how it had ended, but in general with the decline in their communication over the past months. Jonathan, of course, was on the cusp of his wedding, a time that should have been joyous, but he couldn't believe Chris had sprung his estranged mother on him like that. They each knew that they needed to iron out their respective situations, but that night they were going to drink.

Jonathan made his way to the dance floor and started to boogie. His style was weird and kind of awful but fun to watch, and he was dancing with such enthusiasm that it drew a crowd to him. And the crowd wasn't hating; some were amused, but some were genuinely impressed by the way he was moving his arms and legs independently of each other, blowing his lifeguard's whistle along in time with the latest rap hits that the deejay was spinning. Roheed was breakdancing expertly beside Jonathan, a skill he had perfected in the Bay Area to let off steam between long coding sessions while he built apps. Jonathan and Roheed caused quite a scene. At one point, they were doing a "Macarena"-infused "Gangnam Style" dance to Rebecca Black's "Friday."

Charlie sat with Judas in his booth as they drank. Judas, amused, watched Jonathan and Roheed.

Charlie eyed him suspiciously. "How did you know about Jonathan's bachelor party tonight?"

"I sensed it. I can whiff out a bach' par' from miles away," Judas said. Charlie didn't buy it. Judas noticed and relented. "I'm actually in town for a speaking engagement. I was about to step outside for a vape and I saw you chumps rolling up and I knew you weren't going to get in."

Charlie glugged his gimlet.

Judas chuckled. "I haven't seen you guys in forever. When was that whole relay race thing? The summer before last?"

"No, three summers ago." Charlie answered too quickly,

then covered, "I mean, I think, who knows? It's not like I ever think about that stuff." Except that just the night before, he and Jonathan and Roheed had talked for two hours about that very era of their lives.

"Right," Judas said, then scrunched up his forehead as if he was thinking hard. "Hey," he said, raising his voice an octave or two higher, "Are you still mad about my whole 'betraying you all' thing?"

Charlie thought he should be, but found it hard to care anymore. Would he still be working summers at the snack bar if they had flat-out won the Tri-County Relay Race? He hoped not. Would Jonathan still be secretly living there? He wasn't sure. Had Judas maybe done them all a favor? Maybe.

"I think we're cool, man," Charlie said.

Judas smiled. "Cool."

"What have you been up to since then?" Charlie redirected the line of questioning at Judas, who was more than ready to talk about himself.

"Well, I started working at Chain Male," Judas began.

"The store where the mannequins have nipples?"

"And abs!" Judas replied, a little too excitedly. "And I was doing pretty well."

Charlie could tell he was going to be there for a while, so he refilled his drink and listened as Judas painted a picture with his words.

• • •

Judas ran the sales floor of Chain Male, the uber-popular athletic clothing store. His job entailed showing sweat-resistant products to swole bros, fit chicks, and overweight dads who loved sports. He was in shape and knew what he was talking about, which translated to major sales, much to the satisfaction of his manager, Sean Matters, another mid-twenties bro with big biceps.

One day, Sean and Judas were standing by the energy drink refrigerator in the break room, sipping mutagen-green caffeinated beverages, when Sean said he had some news for Judas.

"I'm transferring to Cali bro, they're making me Chain Male regional director of the So-Cal area."

"Bro!" Judas exclaimed excitedly. They bumped forearms in celebration. Judas almost thought a butt pat was in order but refrained.

"They said I could assemble my team, and there's no *ass* I'd rather *emble* than yours, bro. I was wondering if you wanted to go to 'Fornia with me?"

"That sounds epic!" Judas was pumped, but hesitant. "Let me powernap on it and I'll get back to you ASAP."

"V cool, bro, v cool," Sean said, exiting the room.

Judas fist-pumped to himself alone in the break room. He totally wanted to move to California and work with Sean, but he had grown up in Yellow County and didn't know if he wanted to leave quite yet. He was a big fish in a small pond, and a big pond didn't necessarily sound like where he wanted to swim.

He pondered like he had never pondered before as he restocked the men's bikini briefs later that day. By fate, or maybe just by another one of those happenstances that happens to stance in Yellow County, a gentleman with an energetic aura about him floated into the store and across the room to where Judas was working. He had dark hair, an Asian-American flavor about him, and a wisp of a T-shirt covering his impeccable pecs. This earned him a lot of notice from other customers, but Judas was deep in thought, engrossed in his task and his ponderments.

The man walked right up to Judas and said, "Excuse me."

Judas turned, a pair of undies in hand. "Welcome to Chain Male, how can I help you?"

The man looked deep into Judas's eyes. "What can you tell me about the product you're currently holding?"

Judas didn't skip a beat. "The Chain Male luxury men's bikini brief is the Hummer H2 of things that cover your booty. The sweat-resistant material will treat your package like a FedEx carrier on ecstasy. And the elastic waistband does not warp, even if you're going from the gym to the bedroom or the office to the discothèque."

The man just watched and nodded. "Sold," he said, "I'll take every pair of thirty-inch waist you've got."

Judas couldn't believe it. "Bro!"

The man smiled. "Bro."

Judas cleared out the floor and stock room of the particular size of Underoos that the man had requested. He loaded the bags into the back of the man's yellow Hummer H2. The man hit a button on his key fob and the trunk door closed.

Judas gave a little wave. "Thanks!" he said, and turned back toward the store.

"Wait," the man said. "I know talent when I see it. The way you inspired me to buy those briefs, I think you could inspire young adults to be great."

"Huh?"

The man handed Judas his business card. It read, *Gregory Thang: G THANG Motivational Speaking*, and in smaller type, *& Realty*. The slogan underneath read, *When nuthin' but a G Thang will do.*

Judas clasped the card in his hand and watched the G Thang himself peel out of the parking lot in his ridiculously, unnecessarily large vehicle.

Things progressed from there. Judas called the number on the card and Gregory Thang took him on as a protégé in the art of *brotivational* speaking.

At first they just met to work out together. After showering up and talcing down, Gregory would have Judas (they were always standing in the locker room, both still in towels at that point by the way) deliver a speech to himself in the mirror. If you can convince yourself, Gregory would say, you can convince others.

Judas spoke cautiously, thinking about his words before saying them. Gregory would shake his head and ask Judas where the confidence was that he initially saw when Judas sold him those pairs of underwear. Judas took that to heart and brought his frat bro swagger to his message. Soon he was adept in the mirror challenge and was ready to speak to others.

Judas started speaking to frat houses half full of a couple of dudes in popped-collared shirts. He wore Chain Male polos, he amateurishly gelled his hair, and once he got in front of an actual audience, he was nervous again, referring to cue cards sporadically.

"Hello, uh, dudes," he would start. "Today I'm going to be speaking to you about confidence?" he said sheepishly.

But he got better. He stood on the bar at a Case Of The Mondays chain restaurant while waitresses in sexy secretary outfits served wings and beers to schlubby young professionals who had turned up for the advertised speaking engagement. Judas wasn't using cue cards anymore, he had figured out his hair—he used fiber now, not gel—and he had invested in some nice shirts and slacks, not the douchey Chain Male stuff he had been wearing.

"What can confidence get you?" He was still a little hesitant. "Sure, maybe a date with one of these fine waitresses here." He smiled at a waitress who rolled her eyes but then did actually smile in spite of his cheesiness. He just had something, a charisma that kept people listening.

And with time he got good, really good. He spoke to the Brown State Lacrosse Team, their coaches, and the rest of the BS LAX staff. He walked the field, owning it. He was dressed well and had one of those Britney Spears mics projecting his voice to his engaged audience.

"But you know what else confidence can get you?" He had his spiel down pat. "Jobs. Jobs ain't just for Stevie anymore fellas, I'm talking about money in the bank, cash money. Money can buy you things." The dudes in the crowd would murmur and nod their heads.

Judas spoke at the Chain Male regional conference at the Yellow County Convention Center in an enormous room filled with alpha males. He was on stage with buzzwords projected onto a screen behind him as lasers danced around the room. He had grown his hair out to shoulder-length, and the top half was pulled back into a Tom Cruise in *Magnolia* ponytail.

"And things make the world go 'round. What do you have to do to get those things?" The crowd was quiet; Judas had their undivided attention. He whispered, "Stuff." The crowd murmured in approval.

Judas repeated himself at regular volume, "Stuff."

He pumped his fist and yelled, "Stuff! Stuff! Stuff!" and the crowd chanted along with him. He made a motion like a conductor signaling a band to rest. The crowd fell silent.

"So if you take nothing from this talk but one thing, let it be: Have the confidence to do the stuff that will get you things.

Thank you. Goodnight."

Judas waved, the curtain closed, and the crowd went wild. He was crushing it, consistently, and making handfuls of money doing it even though he really wasn't saying much, if anything.

Life was good for Judas the brotivational speaker.

• • •

Charlie was drunk, pretty jealous, and a little confused. "Wow," he muttered.

Judas nodded proudly.

"You're killing it," Charlie said. "Jonathan is probably hopefully still getting married, and Roheed is dating a socialite heiress deejay and making apps. What the hell am I doing with my life?"

Judas shrugged. "I don't know, but I know what we're doing tonight."

Charlie raised his eyebrows to Rude Jude.

Judas paused for dramatic effect, then said, "We're going back to the pool."

CHAPTER 8

THE H2'S DOORS slammed shut. Seatbelts clicked. Judas's foot mashed the pedal to the floor and they were off. Judas, Charlie, Roheed, and Jonathan headed like a speeding bullet straight back to where they had met several summers before. Jonathan was riding shotgun, or "shotty boom ba lotty" as Judas had referred to it, and his emotions were riding a roller coaster. His heart ached to be back at the Yellow County Community Swim and Racquet Club, to smell the smells and stomp once again upon his former stomping ground. His brain told him that it would not be the same—it would never be the same—without Bill. Jonathan would never work at the pool again, he supposed, and that made him sad. But he was excited to visit one more time. Also he was drunk.

Speaking of drunk, Roheed was intoxicated for the first time in his life. He thought it was pretty cool. He had abstained until that evening because he knew that nothing good could come from ingesting alcoholic beverages, but that night was going to have to be a mulligan.

Charlie sat in the backseat with Roheed, wondering if Roheed was going to barf or yak or ralph or call dinosaurs on the big white telephone. He also wondered if Judas was too drunk to drive.

He leaned forward and asked, "Are you cool up there?"

Judas scoffed. "I was in a fraternity, it would take a keg of moonshine and an elephant tranquilizer to slow me down." But still he slowed the Hummer slightly as if Charlie's question had worried him just a bit.

Even though Charlie still lived in Yellow County, he hadn't been to the pool since the Tri-County Relay Race. Jonathan had been fired and humiliated, sure, there were concrete reasons why he wouldn't want to return to the club, but Charlie couldn't pinpoint why he couldn't bring himself to go. If only for an afternoon in the summer when the sun was scorching, a dip in the clear blue of the pool's over-chlorinated water would be mighty fine. The thought of walking through the big green metal doors and past the lovely older gentlewoman who signed you in and rented ping-pong paddles and balls and stepping out into the too-bright sunlight, blinking because your eyes had already adjusted to the dimness of the men's locker room, made Charlie feel sick. It made him feel as if a stranger was giving him a tour of his own childhood home but the furniture was different and there were photographs of a different family hung about the walls and maybe even where his bedroom used to be was a locked door with strange noises coming from behind it. But like Jonathan, he wanted to go that night with those friends.

Judas's H2 roared into the Yellow County Community Swim and Racquet Club parking lot. He parked diagonally across all of the disabled person parking spots. Judas, Jonathan, Charlie, and Roheed got out and gazed in awe at the club.

"I haven't been here since I last left," Jonathan said vaguely, as that could really be said about any place at any time. But they all knew what he meant.

"Me neither," Charlie agreed.

"I was here a month or two ago just chillin'," Judas said obliviously. "They've really stepped up their game since we worked here. I come here all the time when I'm in town during the summer; it's awesome now."

Charlie shook his head. They approached the pool.

Judas wouldn't shut up. "Much, much, *much* better than before . . ."

The next few hours were a blur, mostly due to the booze, but also because they were in and out of the water, laughing at times and silently enjoying the club at times. Judas popped champagne immediately as they broke the threshold from the men's room. They all drank straight from the bottle. They stripped to their undergarments. It was no surprise to anyone that Jonathan was wearing a Yellow County Community College swim team speedo as underwear.

Judas ran and did an impressive flip into the three feet, a big no-no, but no one was there to bench him for his dangerous behavior. Roheed, brash because of the alcohol, climbed up the steps of the newish high dive that had replaced the old soldier. He fearfully walked to the edge of the board, looked down, and decided he was absolutely *not* going to jump. He turned to retreat back down the steps, with their strip of scratchy black tape that during the summer gripped the wet feetsies of those brave enough to climb them. Charlie was there on the board with him. Roheed's mouth opened, and Charlie smiled and pushed Roheed. He fell into the water with a satisfying *sploosh* and a moment later popped to the surface spluttering and laughing. Charlie dove in after him. Judas answered the call of nature and peed down the light blue waterslide. Later he would forget that he had peed down the slide, slide down the slide, then remark how warm the water slide water was, and how it smelled like an outhouse.

As the boys frolicked, Jonathan sat in one of the tall guard chairs, just watching. He took his red lanyard and whistle from around his neck and spun it around his finger one way until it wrapped itself up, then the other way to the same result, and repeated that. It was calming, methodical. He did that for quite some time, sort of in a trance, maybe meditating in his own way. After a while, he calmly climbed off the guard chair, and while Judas and Charlie were throwing Roheed back and forth in the water between them like a sack of sweet potatoes, he walked to the snack bar and let himself in.

He hit a couple of switches on the fuse box and the snack shack sprang to life. With a hiss and a poof, the gas grill flared up. And Jonathan went hog wild. Frozen burger patties hit the hot metal with a satisfying *shhhh* as if they were saying, "Shhhh, don't tell anyone we're cooking, eat all of us yourself." He made a pyramid of perfectly grill-marked hot dogs, he put on a fresh pot o' cheese for nachos, he gave a bag of frozen French fries a bubble bath in hot, golden oil, and he even made a couple of chicken quesadillas, as annoying as they were to make.

Charlie, Judas, and Roheed passed around a bottle of Fireball, which to the uninitiated is a deceptive drink that tastes like an old-school cinnamon jawbreaker but wreaks havoc on your insides and decision-making centers. When the bottle was done, they had thick saliva, sugar headaches, and drunk munchies. The smell from the snack bar wafted down to where they were. They floated up the steps between the chipped dark green-painted handrails like they were anthropomorphic wolves in an old Saturday morning cartoon, being led by a giant hand giving them the come-hither finger motion. Roheed flung open the door and they saw the spread of snacks that Jonathan had prepared.

It was glorious.

They partied and ate until the sun shot out his first warning rays of "Hey, a new day is about to begin, bros!" They stumbled out of the snack bar with ketchup-stained fingers and imitation nacho-flavored non-dairy cheese substitute flecks in their facial hair. Judas left a stack of bills in their wake to pay for the foodstuffs and the extra chemicals that would potentially have to be used to rebalance the pH of the pool.

It was nearly daytime when they packed it in and slunk back to Judas's H2. They drove away just as the off-season pool manager at the time, Devon Wilkenshire, pulled up to open the gate so that the early morning gentlemen's fall volleyball league could get in and play. Devon thought he recognized the crew of apparent trespassers, but then thought, *Nah, no way it was those four dudes.*

CHAPTER 9

EVERYONE WOKE UP hungover, except Judas, who arose at about eight and promptly went to the gym for some cardio. He was built for nights like the night before. Jonathan awoke on the cot in his office still in his bathing suit, upper thighs smelling of pre-mildew, spooning Tim the CPR dummy. His head pounded between his hands as he made his way to the indoor pool and sat on the ladder leading into the deep well area. After a dip, he went to the sauna to try and sweat the evil out. Instead, he barfed on the hot rocks, sending a putrid burst of steam into the chamber. That actually made him feel better, so he went to the on-campus Dave & Buster's and played skee-ball, then walked to the campus dining hall.

Jonathan sat amongst the students, dark sunglasses on, eating scrambled eggs made by Deena, the cafeteria lady. Her recipe was a campus hit: a little bit of cream cheese in the mix, a lot of love, and a medium amount of Maryland seafood seasoning. As he ate, Jonathan wondered what in the heck he was going to do about Chris and the wedding and his mother.

Charlie slept on the floor of his small living room. He used a pool towel as a blanket. Roheed nudged him awake; Charlie grumbled.

"Why does my body hurt so much?" Roheed asked through squinted eyes. "My brain feels like it's dry and my stomach feels like I have to poop vomit."

"Welcome to your first hangover," said Charlie, an old pro in that realm.

"This is awful. Why would anyone repeat the behaviors that cause this?" Roheed was sincerely confused.

Charlie didn't know, but grumpily offered, "Because we're idiots." He picked himself up and exited the room, returning with mason jars of tap water and a couple of aspirin.

"Drink this." He handed a jar to Roheed. "Take these, we'll make BLTs later."

Roheed didn't know why, but BLTs sounded like the exact antidote to his self-poisoning the night before. He drank the water thirstily as Charlie checked his phone, squinting through just one eye. Both of his eyes bugged open as he read a text.

"Jill texted me. She wants to grab lunch. Will you be cool here for a few hours if I go?"

Roheed lowered himself onto the couch. "I don't trust myself to go anywhere right now. I only feel comfortable staying on this couch and watching numerous episodes of a Netflix-produced show for several hours in a row."

"You're going to binge-watch *Bojack* or something?"

"Pardon me?"

"Never mind," Charlie said, and went to shower to try to make himself presentable.

• • •

Charlie drove to the coordinates he had agreed upon with Jill. It was a Case Of The Mondays restaurant within spitting distance of Brown State University. Charlie had grown up going to COT Mondays; there was one in Greenbelt down the road from Beltway Plaza, after all. It was an office-themed chain restaurant where the female servers wore secretary outfits and heels and the guys wore short-sleeved button-down shirts with a pocket protector and neckties. Office paraphernalia was hung on the walls: calendars, productivity signs (Hang in there, baby!), charts, graphs, and *Dilbert* strips. They had gone all out to make their restaurant look like a "fun" office, like anyone who spent an entire workday in a cubicle would want to go get drunk with their coworkers or have a meal with their family at a place that sort of resembled their office. Nonetheless, COT Mondays was popular enough to have several locations in the Tri-County area.

That particular COT Mondays was packed with Brown State students in their bowel-movement-brown Brown State University sweaters and hats and such. Charlie was annoyed for just a moment until he saw Jill sitting sideways in a booth, a book resting on her smooth, tan legs. She was wearing a low-key Brown State polo shirt. It wasn't doo-doo brown like her classmates' apparel, but grey with a small, brown *BS* on the breast. It was size *S* for the *Small* heart attack it was giving Charlie. He breathed, approached the table, and sat.

"You didn't tell me we were meeting at a Brown State hang."

Jill folded the corner of her current page in the book and closed it. She tucked a piece of her mostly pulled-back hair behind her ear. She had it in a ponytail, but loose, and there were a few stragglers making a break for her cheekbones. Charlie thought it was cool that she dog-eared instead of bookmarking. To him, books were meant to get beat up and show their wear. You could tell a good book by its mileage, much like you could tell a life lived well by one's scars and tattoos and wrinkles and laugh lines. Did the reader really read the thing or did it sit on a shelf? Was it reread? Was there a passage in there that you just had to look up every now and then to explain how you were feeling at a moment in time? Were there notes in the margins? Did you highlight anything?

A bookmark was a truce flag, a surrender to an activity other than reading. A dog-ear was a promise—hold my spot; I'll be back with reinforcements as soon as I can.

Jill looked up. "What do you have against Brown State? What has Brown done to you?"

"Brown State, Brown Town," Charlie shrugged. "They're Yellow County's rivals."

Jill smiled. "In what?"

"I don't know—swimming and stuff? I'll admit it's not the most rational disdain, but Brown has always left a bad taste in my mouth."

Jill laughed. "Ew, what?"

Charlie realized how that sounded and joined Jill laughing. He smiled and looked into Jill's eyes. He felt like they had changed color since he had known her those summers before, or at least the color had deepened and there was more behind her eyes now.

"Thanks for texting me," he said.

"It was apparent you weren't going to." *Is there a hint of a smile?* Charlie wasn't sure.

"Yeah, I should have." Charlie looked down at the menu, which was made up to look like a spreadsheet, detailing the item, the ingredients, the calorie count, and the price. *So weird. Why would anyone respond to this?* Charlie thought.

Just when it was getting to the point where no one had said anything and it was about to get awkward, Jill smiled and looked away from Charlie, playing with her hair with her pointer and middle fingers. When she smiled Charlie noticed a small chip in one of her teeth. He liked it. It was a small imperfection on a smile that otherwise could be used on an "after" poster in a dentist's office. An exception that proved a rule.

"It's funny that we're here," she said, the strands of hair dancing between her fingers like a single feather of a rare bird caught in the wind, blowing around a lush meadow. Charlie snapped out of whatever had made him think that series of words and images, and brought himself back to the present.

"Huh? Yeah."

Jill nodded. "You know, I had such a crush on you when we worked in the snack bar."

"Oh really?" Charlie responded sarcastically.

"You knew?" Jill was genuinely surprised.

"I think one time you said you were saving yourself for me."

Jill laughed, embarrassed. "I guess it was obvious. I was a mess back then, so immature."

Charlie grinned. "You landed on your feet."

They shared another moment. The conversation was getting easier. Jill cocked her head down slightly so that she had to look up just a few degrees for her eyes to meet Charlie's, her voice soft as baby cheeks.

"So what have you been up to since our summer in the snack bar, Charlie Heralds?" Charlie's name melted away as it left her lips.

But Charlie was embarrassed and hesitant. "I take a couple credits per semester at YCCC. I work at Popcorn Movies, which is on the brink of bankruptcy, and the only thing I've ever written was stolen by Jerd McKinley."

"Wow," Jill chided. "So you're really winning right now."

"And I'm not seeing anyone currently, obviously, and maybe it's because I'm too honest like this on dates."

Jill's face straightened. "You think this is a date?"

Charlie got flustered, "Oh, I uh . . ."

Jill cracked. "Don't worry," she smiled, "it is."

Charlie was relieved to see the server approaching, dressed as a sexy, but still PG, administrative assistant with a tray with their water cups on it. The cups, though, were the annoying cones that you get from a typical office's water cooler, very impractical for a restaurant. Each paper cone could only hold a couple of ounces of water and came with a metal support ring—it was the worst idea.

"Welcome to Case Of The Mondays!" the server said with forced enthusiasm. "Would you like to start off with any Application-*tizers*?" She cupped her hand to her mouth like she was letting them in on a lil' secret. "That's what we call appetizers here at COTM."

"We're ready to order," Jill said, which sent Charlie scrambling to figure out his order as he hadn't even glanced at the menu, too taken with his former crusher and current crushee's remarkable, dare he say, beauty.

"I'll have the Corporate Ladder Sampler as my meal," Jill said.

"Marinara for the mozzarella sticks?"

"Please." Jill handed the server her menu, a three-ringed binder that said REPORTS in big letters then the name of the restaurant underneath.

"And I'll have the Resume Builder Burger with the, uh, Files? Is that what you call fries? Files?"

The server nodded, wrote down their orders, smiled, and walked away.

"This place is so stupid," Charlie said, looking around the room.

"Yeah, what a terrible idea for a restaurant theme," Jill said with a smile.

Charlie laughed. "Whoever thought of this place is an idiot."

As they continued chatting, the words flowed effortlessly. They caught up on each other's lives over the past handful of years, laughing about the time they spent during their summer together.

Jill and Charlie were so absorbed in each other's words and eyes that neither realized Scott was sitting in the next booth over, a Brown State knit beanie pulled down low over his eyes (well, singular "eye"), his back to Jill's, listening to every word.

CHAPTER 10

ROHEED WAS SPRAWLED out on Charlie's couch, a wet washcloth draped on his forehead, covering his closed eyes. He was massaging his temples when his phone made that awful sound that phones make when a video call is coming through. He answered it. Florence's face popped up on the screen. She saw the state that Roheed was in and laughed.

Roheed was grumpy. "It's not amusing."

"Aw, I'm sorry, 'Heed." Florence did that cute thing where her eyes were smiling but her mouth frowned in an overdramatic display of sympathy. "You just look pretty cute with your little washcloth on your head."

"Anyway," Roheed rolled his eyes, "I did this to myself because of you."

"What?"

"I went out drinking after I saw you with *him*."

"Who?"

"You know who."

She did. "Al? Yeah, he was at the club I played last night, along with three thousand other people."

Roheed was pissed. "Were all three thousand people also your ex-boyfriends? And before you answer, you don't have to, because I'm being facetious. I know you've had significantly fewer ex-boyfriends than that."

Florence was getting heated as well. "If you don't trust me, then I don't need to be talking to you right now. Maybe call me back when you've adjusted your attitude."

"Maybe call *me* back when . . ." Roheed sputtered, "*you've* adjusted *your* . . . uh, gratitude . . ." He searched for words, but like a prop gun in an old Western, he came up blank. "Never mind, my head hurts."

"Green's not your color, babe," Florence said, and then her face disappeared from Roheed's phone with a *whoosh* and a *zoop*.

Roheed wasn't sure if she meant green with envy or that he physically looked green because he felt so sick. It didn't matter. He seriously considered throwing his phone across the room into the wall, but the way his brain worked, it played out a million micro-scenarios and he just couldn't let himself do it. There was no upside except for a brief moment of satisfaction, he reasoned. Instead, he simply set the phone down gently on the floor. Then he lay back on the couch and slid the fuzzy, faded light blue washcloth he had been nursing his headache with down over his face to block out the world.

• • •

Jonathan was sitting in his office polishing his whistle—seriously, that's not a euphemism; he was actually making sure his coach's whistle was nice and shiny. He had a little thing called pride, after all. Chris entered, and even though Jonathan's back was to her, he sensed her presence.

"You should have told me she was coming," he said, not turning to face her.

"Would you have met with her if I did?" Chris asked.

Jonathan thought for a moment. "No."

There was a pause, and then Chris replied, "There you go."

Jonathan did a half-turn in his chair so that Chris could see his profile. He spoke quickly and passionately. "You don't get it, *your* dads are cool. *Your* dads went out of their way to adopt you *and* neither of your dads are even dead. What the h-e-double diving boards?" He got quiet. "My dad, who was my best friend, died, and then my father figure even died. You still have two awesome dads."

Chris pulled up a chair next to Jonathan and put her hand on his shoulder. She could have said a lot of things, but they wouldn't have been helpful in that moment. She could have told Jonathan stories from the orphanage, where the caretakers treated her poorly, and where because she was older than most of the other kids they all said she would never get adopted. She could have told Jonathan about the hoops her dads had to jump through to adopt her because it was "frowned upon" for two men, who couldn't get married at the time, to adopt a child. She could have told him the hateful things her classmates in high school had said to her about her dads and the things people still posted on the internet about the subject. But she didn't; he already knew. And it wasn't the right time to bring those things up again.

Instead, she said, "I know it still hurts, and what your mom did in reaction to your dad's death hurt you, too. But think about it from her perspective. You lost your father. She lost her husband." Jonathan hadn't thought of it that way. Chris continued. "I'm sure if she had it to do over again, she would have done it differently."

"This isn't *Hot Tub Time Machine*, she can't just do it over," Jonathan said sadly, angrily.

Chris tried to stay with the movie references. "But maybe you can forgive her, uh, like in *Unforgiven*."

"I don't think that's the best example of forgiveness, a movie called *Unforgiven*."

"I haven't actually seen it," Chris confessed.

"Me neither."

Chris got back on task. "She'll be at the rehearsal dinner tomorrow night," she offered.

Jonathan was indignant. "Who says I'm going to be there?"

Chris just gave him a look.

"Yeah, I'll be there," Jonathan admitted. "Damn it, I just love your damn self so damn much."

"I love you too, Pooley."

"Can we just like, talk about things from now on? No more surprises?"

Chris nodded. They hugged. It was sweet.

They kissed and kept kissing and then suddenly tongues

were involved and it was a little much. They fell onto the nearby cot and pulled a fuzzy, light blue pool towel over them, size *XL* for the *Xtra Long* lovemaking they were about to do.

• • •

Roheed slid from his face the fuzzy, light blue washcloth that had been keeping his thumping headache at bay. He looked over and saw Charlie sitting at the table with his computer. Charlie was just staring at the screen until he registered that Roheed had stirred.

He adapted a faux-nurturing voice, "How you doing, little buddy?"

Roheed blinked his eyes separately, then together. "My cranium feels like it's less affected by gravity than it usually is."

"You're lightheaded? Yeah, after the hangover and the ibuprofen you'll feel a little woozy."

Roheed steadied himself against the arm of the couch. "Are you back to writing?" he asked.

Charlie prepared to say yes, but then chose honesty. "No. I mean, it's just like before the summer at the pool; I just sit here and I've got nothing."

"What happened with *In Sheep's Clothing*?" Roheed asked. "Why is Jerd McKinley making it into a movie that you have no part of?"

Charlie looked away. "I still don't want to talk about it."

"Yes, you do."

Charlie sighed, "Okay, yeah. I really do." And he began to spin a yarn like a dizzy sweater-knitter.

• • •

Charlie flashed back to his *In Sheep's Clothing* table read. He had held it to hear his words up on their feet and get the opinions of some close friends and family and anyone else willing to spend a couple of hours listening to a very amateur screenwriter's debut attempt. It was held in the Helen Phifer Memorial Auditorium and Musical Studies Annex on the Yellow County Community College campus. Charlie sat at the head of a long table, the chairs filled with actors reading from scripts. A few scattered audience members, including Jonathan, Chris,

Roheed, Florence, and Charlie's parents, Art and Hilda, sat in the stands.

Jerd McKinley was also there, watching intently. He looked exactly how one might think a nerd who created an Internet-based reality web series to get close to the popular girls in school should. His ticker ticked as he listened to Charlie read the scene action from the script.

"Leonora Sheep hangs up the phone." Charlie said, making sure to read slowly and enunciate. "She pulls out her calendar and checks the date the event planner gave her."

An actress read the character Leonora Sheep's lines. "The eighth, why does that date sound so familiar?"

Charlie added some bass to his voice for the next line. "She flips to the eighth and gapes in horror."

The actress had been in several tacky local commercials, including the one where the family is trying to figure out where to eat dinner and they settle on an establishment that serves pizza and fried food and is governed by a large purple ape. "The eighth!" she exclaimed.

She is doing quite well, actually, Charlie thought.

"The eighth is the next full moon. I can't put on a career-launching fashion show. . ." she paused, "if I'm a werewolf!"

If she had been holding a microphone at that moment she would have dropped it, *boom*. But since they didn't have microphones and were just trying to project through the large auditorium, she didn't drop a mic. Instead, she took the blue BIC Round Stic she was using to follow along with her lines and make notes in the margins of the screenplay and placed it down on the table gently.

After the script was read, the audience filed into the adjoining reception hall. Overall, the table read went well enough, Charlie guessed. He didn't want to beat himself up too bad. He was taking baby steps, but this was not what he had envisioned for his life. He guessed that he was relatively young, and this was the first thing he had written, and, admittedly, it did kind of suck and the structure wasn't perfect, but he had put words on the page and done the proverbial damn thing, and *damnit*, he was damn proud of his damn self.

After munching on brownies his mom brought, Charlie asked

for feedback from her, his dad, and his friends. Each offered the obligatory positive but relatively vague feedback: "Great dialogue!" and "Very promising!" and "Did that really take more than two hours? It flew by!" Then, Charlie was approached by who he had thought was a student there at the community college, but in actuality was still a high school student at East Yellow High.

"I have a question," the young man said.

"One second," Charlie responded, saying to his friends, "Thanks again for coming. I hope to see you again soon. Come into Popcorn Movies whenever. I can get you free rentals."

They said their goodbyes and walked away, leaving Charlie with the young man.

"Yes?"

"You were delving into some pretty complex themes. I was wondering how you were able to relate so well to a werewolf."

And just like any artist at any stage in their creative life, no matter how newly burgeoning, Charlie began to wax poetic. "You see," he began pretentiously, "I, too, used to have a secret I kept, much like the protagonist of my screenplay. I have webbed toes."

But the young man cut him off, sensing that Charlie could potentially go on for a while if not reined in and kept on track. "How is having webbed toes like being a werewolf?"

"It's a metaphor," Charlie replied.

"For what?"

Charlie thought for a moment. "Like shame, I guess?"

"Sure," the fellow said. "Anyway, I thought the script was pretty cool."

"Thanks." Charlie finally recognized whom he was speaking to. "Aren't you the *Rich B Words* guy?"

"Jerd McKinley." Jerd stuck out his hand for a shake. "Florence invited me. She knows I'm into this kind of thing."

Charlie obliged, extending his hand. "Thanks for coming."

And with that, he thought the conversation was probably done—or close to it—so he shifted his weight to go get another one of his mom's brownies, but Jerd surprised him by saying, "Hey."

Charlie stopped.

"So, I'd love to develop this script with you."

"Really?" Charlie scanned Jerd's face with his built-in *BS*-o-meter and the reading came back negatory.

Jerd continued, "I've made some connects through *Rich B Words* out in Hollyweird and I bet we could get this thing made."

"That would be awesome." Charlie had written the script expressly for the purpose of being discovered, like those *Good Will Hunting* boys his aunt brought up every Thanksgiving, and whisked away to Hollywood to write movies. But he had never thought that it would happen so soon.

He was already daydreaming about what actors would play which roles and wondering what snacks would be at the craft services table on set when Jerd said, "Yeah, it will. Send me the document and I'll send you some notes."

Charlie was still in a far-off, palm tree-lined world. "Wow, okay."

Jerd and Charlie shook hands again; this time, Charlie was more excited about it. Jerd turned to walk away but stopped one last time.

"Oh yeah," he said, as casually as a cat in comfy pajamas, "go ahead and send me the Final Draft document."

Charlie was confused. Final Draft was the screenwriting software he had used to write the script. If Jerd had that version of the document, the original .FDX file, he could make edits to it himself instead of Charlie, cleaning up any commas, or run-on sentences—Lord knows he wrote a run-on sentence or two. But why wouldn't Jerd be satisfied with a read-only PDF?

"Won't a PDF be fine?" Charlie asked.

"Nah," Jerd replied. "I'd prefer the .FDX."

"It'll have to be an .FDR," Charlie said reluctantly. "I have an older version of the program."

Jerd smiled. "That's fine. I can upconvert."

Charlie was optimistic despite the minutiae of what kind of file he would be sending. Jerd walked away confidently while Charlie watched with a look on his mug like he had just won the life lottery.

Charlie did, indeed, send Jerd the .FDR file of his *In Sheep's Clothing* script. He sent a PDF as well, as a subtle reminder to Jerd that he should look but not touch.

The very evening Jerd received the email with the aforementioned attachments, he went to work. He sat in his dark bedroom clacking on his keyboard and cackling like a kooky caveman. He erased Charlie's name entirely off the title page of the script. The cursor blinked for a moment. Then his fingers did some walking and his name, *Jerd McKinley*, popped onto the page. He sipped from a Mountain Dew as he made the monumental Mountain Don't.

CHAPTER 11

ROHEED COULDN'T BELIEVE the tall tale that Charlie was telling. But then again, he kinda could; things in Yellow County had a way of happening *happenstantially*. They sat in Charlie's living room, Charlie looking dejected, seemingly at a stopping point in his story.

"What happened after that?" Roheed implored.

"Ah, you don't want to hear the rest, do you?"

Roheed just about leapt across the coffee table. "Finish the story!"

"Okay, okay," Charlie said. "Hold your horses."

Roheed relaxed a tad.

Charlie got back into narrating mode. "For a while, not much happened on the *In Sheep's Clothing* front. I just assumed that the opportunity had gone away. Until . . ."

• • •

Charlie was working at the local Popcorn Movies video rental joint. Outside, a MovieVend movie vending machine had been callously set up by the drugstore next door. On his shifts, Charlie would watch dozens of people rent movies from the automated box instead of coming inside his store for a better selection and some human interaction. It bummed Charlie out big time.

One day, his coworker Anfernee ran up to the register from the break room. He was carrying his phone, laughing, and dabbing at the corner of his mouth with a napkin to wipe away a bit of whatever he had been munching on during his short break. Whatever had propelled him from his moment of leisure and re-snack-sation had been too pressing for him to stop and compose himself before running to share it with Charlie.

"Yo, Chaz! You gotta see this!" Anfernee exclaimed.

Charlie snapped out of his daze. "What's up?" he squinted, looking towards the screen of Anfernee's phone.

"A clip from *Rich B Words* is going viral, like right now." Anfernee held his phone close to Charlie's face.

On Anfernee's phone's screen, a clip played. In the clip, one of the *Rich B Words* girls (not coincidentally, due to her Jerd connection, she would be the actress that Charlie would see later with Roheed in the *In Sheep's Clothing* movie trailer) was holding a very old pug dog. The girl was as good-looking as the pug was fugly, and this was one fugly pugly. In other words the girl was super-hot.

In the clip, the young woman was sitting with Florence and a couple of other *Rich B Words* cast members. They were all chatting and barely eating their fancy salads and sipping on daytime cocktails. Innocently, the girl held up her hand to her nose; she felt a sneeze coming on.

"Ah, ah, ah choo . . ." *pllbbtttt*. She sneezed and it made her fart at the same time. The very old pug's eyes bulged.

Anfernee almost dropped the phone, he was laughing so hard. "She *snarted*," he said through tears and heaving shoulders.

Charlie was just confused. "What did I just watch?" he asked, suddenly feeling older than he hoped he should.

"History in the making," Anfernee replied.

He dragged the cursor on the timeline back to the beginning and watched the video clip again . . . and again and again.

• • •

Charlie pulled out his phone and showed Roheed that the snart video had millions of views on YouTube.

Roheed watched the video once through and nodded. "I see the appeal of that particular sequence of events."

Charlie continued, "That clip from Jerd's show broke records. It was played on *The Soup, The View, The Stew, The Daily Show, The Yearly Show, Ellen, Fallon, Smellen, Gallon, Goofus and Gallant, The Late Show, The Early Show, The Girlie Show,* and *Pontius Tonight.* That young lady got a book deal off that snart."

Charlie showed Roheed the Amazon link to the girl's book.

Roheed read the title aloud, *"Lean In: So You Can Snart."*

Charlie was already typing into his browser to show Roheed another link. "A T-shirt line . . ."

Charlie held his phone up and Roheed saw a webpage full of T-shirts for sale with catch phrases like "Let's Get It Snarted In Here," "Oops! I Snarted Again," and "Snart Happens When You Party Naked."

"Even a line of frozen dinners," Charlie said, as he once again clicked through to a webpage, this one showing Snart Ones frozen dinners in varieties like "Pork & Beans, beans . . .", "Macaroni and Who Cut the Cheese?", and "Who Beefed? Stroganoff."

Roheed listened to the whole thing politely, giving Charlie his time. When Charlie appeared to be finished, Roheed said, "I know the snart well. Florence began her deejay career off the popularity of that snart. But what does any of this have to do with Jerd and *In Sheep's Clothing?*"

Charlie was worked up, nearly perspiring. *"Rich B Words* blew up. Everyone wanted to see if that girl was going to snart again. How would the pug react to another snart? Would anyone else do two or more bodily functions at once? Doors were opened for the whole cast and especially Jerd. He got general meetings at all the agencies in Los Angeles."

Charlie was building to something and Roheed knew it, but he couldn't put together the puzzle pieces as fast as Charlie was throwing them down.

Charlie continued, "And what was the only writing sample Jerd had to his name when Hollywood came calling?"

Roheed understood it all now. *"In Sheep's Clothing,"* he whispered.

Charlie nodded.

"Wow." Roheed was floored. He was also impressed by Charlie's storytelling abilities. *Maybe this kid does have a future.*

"It really makes me think," Charlie said, gazing out the

window. "Is the script good enough to get made? Or would it never have been good enough and the only reason it will see the light of day is because Jerd stole it?"

"What are you going to do?" Roheed asked.

"Nothing." Charlie looked back at Roheed, a little too intensely for Roheed's liking. "There's nothing I can do. And it really sucks because I had this backup plan where if I couldn't get anyone in Hollywood to read the script I would write it as a novel and try to get it made into a movie that way."

"Is that something that happens?"

"Probably not," Charlie chuckled darkly. "Sitting on my computer is a worthless half-started novelized version of *In Sheep's Clothing*. I mean, how sad. I have one idea and I keep writing it over and over in different formats."

That sounded pretty cool to Roheed, actually. "I would like to read it," he said.

Charlie half-smiled. "Thanks, dude. I'll send you the PDF when I'm finished—if I ever finish."

"I'd prefer a Word document," Roheed said. Charlie was about to be pissed, but Roheed was grinning. "Get it? Like how Jerd stole the script from you?"

Charlie nodded. He got it.

CHAPTER 12

SCOTT SAT IN a puffy chair in his mom's basement trying to look through a View-Master. He tried his good eye on the left side, but no action. Then he tried the right. It wasn't working for him. He threw the View-Master on the floor, where it bounced and rolled next to a broken Nintendo Virtual Boy and a book of Magic Eye pictures. To occupy his time, he pulled out his phone and started scrolling, scrolling, scrolling like good ol' Freddy Durst. He landed on a social media post from none other than Jonathan Poole announcing his and Chris's rehearsal dinner the next night. Scott eyed the post and started to *think, think, think* like an evil Winnie the Pooh.

Yes, it was annoying that Yellow County Community College had bested Brown State in that particular swim meet, but his distaste for Jonathan went deeper. He blamed Jonathan for *the incident*. He had enjoyed attending the Yellow County Community Swim and Racquet Club growing up, but after *the incident* he could no longer go. Instead of blaming his mother, who had dictated that rule, or himself, for doing what he did, he blamed Jonathan. He was going to get Jonathan and Jonathan's loved ones back. He smiled a sickly smirk.

A cloud covered the moon, a cat screeched, and somewhere, in the blackness of the night, a frog farted.

• • •

Jonathan and Chris had rented out Ben's, the popular chili-dog joint downtown, for their rehearsal dinner. A sign out front read, *Poole & Partee Rehearsal Dinner1*. The *1* should have been an *!*. Guests began to arrive around the appointed hour. Of course, Roheed was there, Jonathan's mom Tammy, Chris's two dads Bill and Ted, local estate lawyer Kenneth Strangleman, Matt Hedge, and a few other swimmers on the YCCC swim team. Judas had arrived early and was already drunk and hitting on a waitress.

Charlie and Jill walked in together. Jill's thumb and pointer finger loosely held onto Charlie's pinky as they sort of held hands—but not really.

"Thanks for bringing me as your date," Jill said, looking down at the floor.

"You think this is a date?"

Jill looked up questioningly but saw Charlie's sly smile. She smiled back. Across the room, Roheed's phone started buzzing. His phone was on vibrate, the only respectable way for a phone to be at such a function. It was Florence trying to FaceTime with him. He ran outside into the Washington, DC, dusk to take it.

"Florence!" he huffed. But when the image appeared on the screen it was just the inside of Florence's pocket. Apparently she had butt-FaceTimed Roheed by accident. Roheed ended the connection and tried to FaceTime her back. No answer. He tried to call her again—no answer. But Florence's voicemail message played. Her disembodied voice sang a close version of the *Seinfeld* song, *"Believe it or not, Florence isn't at home, please leave a message at the beep. I must be out, or I'd pick up the phone. Where could I be? Believe it or not, I'm not home."*

Roheed left a message. "Florence, hello, Florence? Are you there? You just butt-FaceTimed me." He waited for her to pick up, to realize her mistake, so they could have a laugh about the miscommunication. No answer. No pardon from the governor.

Roheed was about to hang up, which wouldn't feel nearly as satisfying as if he had an old-school phone with a receiver and a cord and everything so he could slam the earpiece down forcefully, but instead he saw red.

"You know what?" he fumed. "How appropriate that you butt-FaceTimed me because you're being a big-time buttface. You should be here at Jonathan's rehearsal dinner—with me. Not out gallivanting with a goofus like Alabaster Sixx. You should tell that goofus to hoof it and gallivant with a gallant like me. I'll be here in Yellow County with my best friends. There will be other deejay gigs, but this is important. And furthermore . . ."

The voicemail lady cut in like an unwanted dance partner at a middle-school Sadie Hawkins. "If you are satisfied with your message, press one. If you would like to rerecord your message, press two." Although satisfied was most certainly not the way that Roheed felt about his message, he pressed *1* and walked back into the restaurant.

The party guests sat at several long tables that had been pushed together to create the Voltron of tables (or Megazord, depending on your giant robot of choice). Drink cups and paper plates in red baskets and crumpled up napkins festooned the crinkled tablecloths. Jonathan and Chris sat at the head of the table, beaming; they were in their own little world together. Their party that evening was low-key, simple, easy. It felt like *them* to them. The night was almost over and it had gone off without a hitch and Jonathan was thinking about standing to say a few words and probably bid adieu to the folk gathered, when the sound of a metal spoon *ting*ing against a glass quieted the roar of the guests' conversations.

Tammy stood. Her eye makeup had been inexpertly done for the occasion. She looked a little unsteady, like she had been drinking, or maybe she was just that nervous. All the eyes in the room drifted to her faster than a neon-lit Nissan on the streets of Tokyo. Jonathan's reflex was to stand and stop whatever was about to happen, but Chris put a firm hand on his thigh and squeezed. Jonathan relented and remained seated. He felt like Hayden Christensen in that movie where terrible things were happening all around him but he couldn't move or speak properly—you know, *Star Wars: II*.

"Hello, I'm Tammy, Jonathan's mother," she began. Dead silence filled the room. "They say to start your speech with a joke, so here it goes—my ability to be a mother." She smiled with her mouth but her eyes were full of sadness. Tyra Banks would call it the opposite of a "smize"—maybe a "frize" or a "frad." Jonathan's jaw dropped. Chris looked around nervously.

"Get it?" Tammy said to no one and everyone. "I was a joke of a mother to Jonathan. I make Mama June look like Gwyneth Paltrow. I make Dina Lohan look like Martha Stewart. If there were an Olympic event for being a bad mother, they wouldn't even let me compete, because I've already given up my amateur status."

A few awkward chuckles rippled through the crowd.

Tammy wasn't done. "And now I just show up for his wedding? I must have some nerve, right?" She paused. "Wrong. I'm a coward. That's why I didn't even reach out for the past couple of decades. That's why it took Jonathan's soon-to-be-wife tracking me down and convincing me to come, because I know what I did is unforgiveable. And as much as I wish that I had a hot tub time machine like in that movie—I forget what it's called at the moment—I don't have a hot tub time machine. Or even a regular time machine. Or even a regular hot tub. But, for what it's worth . . ." She looked full on at Jonathan, who tried to avoid eye contact but couldn't, ". . . I'm proud of the young man that you've become, son. You didn't need me; in fact, you've done better without me. And the woman you're going to marry tomorrow is a keeper."

She turned her sad smile toward Chris for a moment, and then looked back to Jonathan. "And your dad would be proud."

She sat. There was silence. Jonathan was dumbfounded.

Then a slow clap began, or what some thought was a slow clap at first. It was actually Roheed clapping Kenneth Strangleman on the back because he was choking on his chili-dog.

CHAPTER 13

THE PARTY NEVER quite recovered after Tammy's toast. Friends continued to mingle, chili-ing their dogs and partaking in celebratory beverages, but there was the ever-looming elephant in the room. Chris and her dads talked in hushed voices while Jonathan made sure Strangleman was okay. Roheed walked up to the table where Charlie and Jill were sitting, Jill's hand casually on Charlie's knee.

"Hello friends," Roheed said apologetically. "I don't mean to defecate on the festivities but I'm going to head home."

Jill made a cute frowny face. "Aww."

"We were going to ride together," Charlie said.

"I'll take mass transit. I'd like time to think anyway."

Charlie shrugged. "If you want."

Roheed nodded.

Jill called out "Be safe!" after him as he left the joint. Roheed walked toward the McPherson Square metro station, deep in thought. Scott sidled out of the shadows and followed him. Scott wasn't the stealthiest tracker, but Roheed was so wrapped up, thinking and overthinking his message to Florence, that he didn't notice his tail. He got on the Orange Line headed towards New Carrolton. The conductor garbled over the PA something about the next stop being Metro Center in a voice that sounded like a drunk alien was speaking Chinese on a speakerphone underwater. Scott got on the next car and watched Roheed through the dirty glass that separated the train's segments.

• • •

Back at Ben's, Tammy was sitting by herself, picking at the carcass of a half-eaten chili-veggie dog. She felt a hand on her shoulder. It was Jonathan.

"Hey," he said.

"Hey," she said.

"Can we go for a walk?" Jonathan gestured with his head ever so slightly toward the street that lay outside.

Tammy nodded.

They walked down a sparsely populated Washington, DC, street. Natty Boh beer signs hung in liquor store windows. Drum-heavy go-go beats thumped from car stereos. Jonathan and Tammy's faces were alternately bathed in the green then yellow then red of traffic signals.

"What you said in there, it was . . ." Jonathan began, slowly. "Well, I was going to say it was nice, but that's not really what it was. It was true for the most part, and pretty funny in a weird way." He thought about how he was going to end the statement he had bungee-jumped into. "I guess I'm trying to say thanks for saying it, whatever *it* was."

Tammy stopped, causing Jonathan to stop as well, and she looked into his eyes. "I really am sorry, Jonathan."

Jonathan looked away, down the street into the distance. "I guess I know that."

Tammy continued to look squarely at Jonathan while Jonathan avoided her gaze. "I want to be in your life."

"I haven't had you in my life for too long," Jonathan said, turning to meet Tammy's stare. "I don't need you in my life."

Jonathan hadn't meant that to hurt, but it did, and Tammy looked down at the ground, stinging.

Jonathan continued, "But maybe we can try. We can try some lunches and maybe some dinners after that. Potentially a breakfast at some point."

"It would mean a lot if we could try a lunch."

There was a pregnant pause. When the water broke, Jonathan asked, "Where do you even live by the way?"

"Bowie," Tammy answered. Jonathan opened his mouth to respond, but Tammy shook her head. "I know, I know. It's temporary."

"I guess we could meet at the Town Center," Jonathan sighed. "They have a DuClaw there."

Tammy smiled. "I would like that."

And knowing it was the right thing to do, Jonathan said, "And heck, you should probably come to the wedding, too."

Tammy's face lit up—literally—from red to green, because a traffic signal changed at that very moment. But still, she looked pretty happy too. "Oh, Jonathan!" she said, and she gave him a big hug.

Although he was trying to hold it in, Jonathan kind of smiled a little before giving her a one-armed hug back and then emancipating himself from her grip.

Jonathan wasn't sure where the dust would settle on this newfound relationship with his mother. His wound was gaping, unhealed, but at that time out there on the sidewalk he wasn't worrying about it. She was his mother, and even his hardened heart couldn't fight the preprogrammed nature of that relationship.

"Chris and I were going to go by the venue tonight and drop off some stuff, and if you want to you can come."

"I'd be honored," she said. "What's the venue?"

"The Yellow County Community College Chapel."

"Sounds wonderful."

They continued walking down the street in a comfortable quiet.

• • •

The party was winding down. Charlie and Jill were still at their table, chatting. She was so close he could smell her, but she wasn't wearing perfume. She had a naturally sweet scent with maybe even a little bit of sweat mixed in there. It was as if that smoky, wafty, come-hither hand from the cartoons was grabbing his nostrils and gently tugging him towards her. He was high on her and also a little buzzed from the Miller High Life he had been drinking . . . or was it Miller High Lives? He wasn't sure.

". . . and we were all stressed out and rushing around and I looked over and you had spilled one of those big tubs of ranch dressing."

"I remember that," Jill laughed.

"And you were like looking back over your shoulder like you were trying to be sexy and you dipped your finger in the ranch and licked it off."

Jill continued laughing and shook her head. "I know, I know."

Charlie was laughing too. "But yeah . . ." he breathed, "That summer was great."

"Sure." Jill checked her phone. "Oh man, I have to go. I have some Brown State Swim Team official business to attend to."

"Really? This late?"

"Yeah, I'm not sure what it is. Scott has me drive him around sometimes, you know, he's got just the one . . ." She pointed to her eye.

Charlie flinched. "Yeah. Yeah. Totally. Go for it. I'll pick you up tomorrow for the wedding?"

Jill nodded and smiled as she stood. They exited together. Charlie walked Jill to her car, and this time they weren't playing finger hockey or just holding pinkies or grazing palms, they were assuredly, one hundred percent holding hands. They reached her parking spot. Charlie smiled because she had a "Snart Happens" bumper sticker on the back of her car. Jill walked halfway around to the driver's side but stopped and came back.

"I know how much we love the 'you think this is a date?' joke," she said, "but tomorrow is definitely a date."

She closed her eyes and tilted her head slightly, leaning up to Charlie, and they kissed. It was just for a moment, but it was a good moment, and he closed his eyes with her and nearby a traffic light turned, bathing them in a soft red glow. Their lips parted. Charlie smiled like a goof.

"Definitely," Charlie said dreamily.

Jill sashayed to her car and got in and left and all Charlie could do was watch. Then he floated away to wherever his car was parked and he didn't even remember where that was. He eventually remembered that he had Hitched there so he took out his phone and within a few minutes the same driver from before, Armando, picked him up and they were on their way back to Yellow County.

• • •

Roheed walked in the general direction of Charlie's apartment, away from the Yellow County Community College Campus metro station. Scott rode up the escalator from the station and followed Roheed ominously, not running but moving quickly, like Michael Myers, you know, from *Austin Powers*. He caught up with Roheed easily.

"Give me your phone," he said.

Roheed jumped. "What? What's going on?"

"Give me your phone."

Roheed looked into the relative darkness. "Aren't you the eye—I mean *guy*, from the swim meet?"

Scott just motioned for Roheed to hand over his phone. Roheed obliged, cautiously. Scott immediately threw it as far as he could and it clattered on the sidewalk somewhere and bounced into some reeds.

"That was probably unnecessary," Roheed said.

"Where is that clown Jonathan's wedding going to be?" Scott menaced.

Usually Roheed would have folded like an origami crane but he had kind of a nothing-left-to-lose attitude at the moment. "The address was in my phone," he said. Scott grabbed him by the collar, but he persisted. "I'm not going to tell you."

"That's fine," Scott said casually. He let Roheed go only to pull back his fist and punch Roheed right in the eye, leveling him. Roheed fell to his knees, clutching his face. The sudden jolt of pain woke him up to the reality of the situation.

"Do you wanna tell me now?" Scott sneered. He cocked back his fist for another blow.

Roheed had a brief out-of-body experience. *Hmm, this sucks,* he thought, as he watched himself be throttled by the big goon who had a firm grasp on his shirt once again. Time slowed and he thought about how to escape the situation. He realized that there was nothing he could really do, so he relented and said, "The chapel."

Scott smiled. He thought he was going to have to ask Jill

for info on the whereabouts of Jonathan's wedding and risk her blowing his cover. But pummeling this nerd was easier and less dicey. Sure, she would still be his wheelwoman, but she didn't have to know in-depth what he was up to.

"What are you going to do?" Roheed asked, looking up from his knees. A little bit of blood was making its way into his eyeball, the red tendrils reaching out to touch his deep coffee-colored iris.

"Oh nothin'," Scott lied. "Probably just a little redecorating. Don't worry about it, in fact, just worry about staying put and counting to a hundred before you even think about moving." And with that he took off, laughing.

Roheed looked around in disbelief. He supposed that he had better start counting. "One, two, three, four, five . . ."

• • •

Charlie sat in the Yellow County Community College library with his laptop. The stacks were empty and dark. His screen illuminated his focused face as he clacked away at the keys.

Armando had dropped him off at his apartment. He hadn't seen Roheed there and he was a little buzzed, but inspired. He grabbed his portable computer and raced to the library. If he had taken a slightly different route through campus he would have stumbled upon Roheed counting—"sixty-one, sixty-two, sixty-three . . ." *Happenstantially*, Charlie had decided to go by the Gladys Noon Spellman Fountain in the middle of the quad because it was pretty at night.

He was writing like a madman, fully engrossed in putting words on the page, something he hadn't done in a long time.

• • •

Chris took Suitland Parkway to get back to Yellow County from Ben's. Jonathan rode shotgun while Tammy sat in the backseat. She was leaning forward and talking excitedly to Chris about the wedding. Jonathan was halfway between annoyed and tickled pink, so somewhat of an itchy orange.

"What are your wedding colors?" Tammy asked.

"Blue and white," Chris replied. "Just like the umbrellas at the pool."

Tammy closed her eyes for a moment to remember the vista of the YCCSRC, umbrellas and all. "That sounds simply wonderful."

"I wanted to have chocolate ice cream tacos instead of a cake," Jonathan added, "but Chris vetoed that idea."

"You can have chocolate ice cream tacos every other day of your life, if you want," Chris said.

Jonathan, feeling just the slightest bit playful, winked to Tammy, for the first time in his life, and said, "And I do."

They shared a smile.

• • •

Jill pulled up outside of the Yellow County Community College Chapel. Scott had texted her to meet him there. She was confused; where was he? But there were lights on and movement inside the chapel. She'd wait.

Roheed was still standing in the middle of campus, counting out loud, "Ninety-eight, ninety-nine. . ." He took a deep breath. "One hundred." Then he took off running.

Charlie continued to work, words appearing on the page faster than they ever had before. He had the *In Sheep's Clothing* Final Draft document up (still .FDR, he hadn't upgraded yet) on the right side of his screen and Word open on the left. He was converting the screenplay-formatted text on the right into a competent, if not a little verbose and with a run-on sentence here and there, prose as he novelized his own movie script.

• • •

Chris's car drove onto the Yellow County Community College Campus. Chris, Jonathan, and Tammy were content and chatting easily inside the vehicle. They had no idea how the next hour was going to impact their lives forever.

CHAPTER 14

JILL THOUGHT SCOTT was a little creepy. She initially interviewed for the task of Brown State Swim Team manager with Scott as he was the team captain. She found it difficult to look him in the face, but she forced herself to in spite of the totally groadie scar tissue that train-tracked around his ocular region. But that wasn't all of it. He could be mean, too. He had a nasty temper, to the point that Jill thought that he probably had some undiagnosed rage issues.

One time, in the locker room, a Brown State swimmer had snapped another swimmer's butt with a wet towel. The intended snappee dodged the attack and instead the towel grazed Scott's leg. It took the whole relay race team and their backup anchor to pull Scott off the towel snapper. He had wrapped the towel around the young man's neck and was pulling it tight and threatening to make him eat his own swim cap.

Scott was reprimanded behind closed doors, but didn't even have to step down as team captain. Jill wondered if he knew someone who knew someone.

When Scott isn't angry, he's decent guy, Jill thought. He always reimbursed her for the gas money that it took to drive him around on official Brown State swim business. He got her a good deal on BSST merch from the campus bookstore. And of course, that one time she got too drunk at a frat party and he randomly passed her walking back to her car, he convinced her not to drive, let her crash in his dorm room on the couch, and didn't try any funny business. He even took her to Brown Hot Bagels the next morning and bought her breakfast.

Running a couple of errands was the least she could do for a guy with poor depth perception.

But that night she had been waiting for too long. She called Scott for a status update.

"Hello?" he answered.

"Where are you?" Jill said. "I'm outside the chapel."

"Turn off your lights and park around back. I'm still going to be a few minutes," Scott sneered.

"What's going on? This is for the swim team?"

"It most certainly is," he assured her.

"Well . . . hurry up." Jill said, but Scott had already ended the call.

• • •

Roheed burst into Charlie's apartment. He was sweating and breathing in short ragged bursts. It was apparent to him very quickly that no one was home, especially when he saw the note on the table in Charlie's unmistakable, third-grade-esque, printed handwriting that read: *Inspired. Writing at the library if you need me.*

Roheed caught his breath, wiped his brow, and headed back to the Yellow County Community College campus, where he had just come from.

• • •

There was a full moon that night; appropriate, considering the subject matter of Charlie's movie script, *In Sheep's Clothing*, and also appropriate because things were about to get downright wacky.

Outside the chapel, Chris's car pulled up to where Jill's was only moments before. Around the corner of the chapel, Jill was watching the snart video for, like, the thousandth time. She didn't notice Chris's car parking and Chris, Jonathan, and Tammy exiting the automobile and heading towards the chapel.

Charlie was still at the library, typing like one of those proverbial monkeys on one of those proverbial typewriters. Roheed burst into the large, open room where Charlie was and startled him. Charlie hit save on his word processing software and looked up.

"Whoa there, little buddy," he said. Then he saw Roheed's blackening eye. "What happened to your face?"

Roheed was out of breath. "A black eye . . . from the eye guy."

"What?"

"That Brown State swimmer." Roheed leaned against a bookshelf of young adult literature. A drop of sweat fell off his brow onto a well-read copy of *The Magician's Nephew*. "Scott, I believe."

"He punched you?" Charlie couldn't believe it. How could someone punch Roheed?

"And disposed of my phone. He said he was going to redecorate Jonathan's wedding."

"Jonathan's wedding at the chapel?" Charlie gasped.

"Yeah." Roheed knew, and he knew Charlie knew he knew, so it was weird that Charlie had said that bit of exposition out loud.

"You can see it from here," Charlie said.

They ran over to the large window overlooking YCCC's quad. The window took up the majority of that side of the building to make up for the lack of windows on the other three sides, per the original intended use for the building as Cell Block D of the East Yellow County Correctional Facility. Chris, Jonathan, and Tammy were approaching the chapel. Jill's car was parked around on the other side.

"What's Jill doing at the chapel? She said she was doing Brown State business," Charlie said, and then exchanged glances with Roheed. Without saying anything more, they took off running out of the library.

• • •

Chris, Jonathan, and Tammy entered the chapel, expecting to see it set up for the wedding the very next day. But when they entered, Chris gazed around, unable to comprehend what she was seeing. Jonathan thought that there must have been some sort of mistake, and Tammy thought that she didn't really know her son that well and that he had terrible taste if that was how the wedding chapel was supposed to be decorated.

Once she realized that something fishy was afoot, Tammy could tell that the chapel had been decorated beautifully. There were white and blue flowers, ornate ribbons, and even candles and a yellow carpet leading to the front of the room where the vows were meant to have been said. But now it looked like Andrew W.K. had partied there harder than he'd ever partied before. The flowers were trampled. The candles were broken. The carpet and the ribbons were ripped from their places and tossed aside.

Jonathan's eyes followed the yellow carpet road to where Scott sat on an overturned pew on the chapel's stage, wedding cake smudged on his Brown State T-shirt, size *XL* for the *Xtra Large* amount of carnage he had wrought in the Yellow County Community College Chapel. He had a switchblade in one hand and he was gouging out one of the eyes of the groom wedding cake topper. He looked up at the trio with fire in his eye—the look of insanity. Tammy was no longer happy that she had come along; she now wondered if the wedding would happen at all. In fact, she wondered if they were going to make it out of the chapel unscathed.

The words "Oh my!" escaped Tammy's lips as Scott flicked his wrist and one of the eyes of the groom wedding cake topper popped out and rolled across the floor, coming to rest at her feet. She felt sick.

CHAPTER 15

"Oh no, he did *not* ruin my wedding," Chris said, mostly to herself, as she charged the front of the chapel where Scott was standing. Jonathan grabbed her by the arm and held her back. She could have twisted free easily with the anger-strength she had pulsing through her body, but Jonathan's semi-calm touch rocked her back to reality. She remembered that a potentially dangerous gentleman holding a switchblade was directly threatening them. So, she slowed her roll.

"Calm down, honey," Jonathan said to Chris. Then he turned to Scott, "What the freaking heck, Scott!"

Scott just laughed.

"You know this is where we were supposed to have our wedding, right?" Jonathan barked. "Like, you did this on purpose, to us specifically?" He couldn't wrap his mind around the concept.

Charlie and Roheed burst in and quickly assessed the scene.

"Not cool," Charlie said quietly. He and Roheed fell in line with Jonathan, Chris, and Tammy.

Scott still stood across the room, groom wedding cake topper still in hand, the eye of it freshly gouged. He began walking the chapel stage dramatically, as if he had a soliloquy prepared.

"They say an eye for an eye leaves the whole world blind," he blustered, "and I'm blind all right, blind with rage. And I'm here to collect my pound of flesh." He banged his shin on an overturned pew. "Ah, goshdaggit!"

Charlie whispered to Roheed, "It's the depth perception." Roheed nodded knowingly. Scott hopped around holding his shin in anguish.

"Is this about the swim race?" Jonathan asked. "Is that why you've ruined our wedding?" Jonathan sort of remembered that Scott and Matt Hedge had probably tied in their most recent meet, but that Matt had received the first-place ribbon.

"The swim race?" Scott scoffed. "The swim race was just the decorative groom on a wedding cake of despise and hatred. No, our origin story goes back far before the swim race." Scott got an almost wistful look in his eye.

• • •

Scott flashed back to the Yellow County Community Swim and Racquet Club locker room, many moons ago. Jonathan was about ten years old and he and some other pre-tweens were having a soap hockey scrum in the communal shower area. The boys kicked around a pearl-colored bar of soap, guffawing and jostling as they tried to score a goal against the tile wall.

Young Scott, several years younger than the other boys, watched with two bright eyes, both working—two fully functioning windows to the soul. He was thin, small for his age. He entered the fray.

"Hey," Scott said, too quietly. "Can I play?"

No response. No one heard him; they were caught up in their soap hockey match.

"Excuse me," Scott tried again. Nothing.

There was no malice intended by the playing pals, they simply could not hear Scott's meek words. Scott edged closer, hoping to catch the eye of one of the boys who would undoubtedly ask him to join in. At that moment, another boy checked Jonathan up against the wall. Jonathan's heel kicked the soap bar and it went flying—right into Scott's left eye. Scott hit the floor, hand pressed to his eye, too stunned to cry out. One of the young lads retrieved the soap and everyone went back to playing the game, not noticing that Scott was in pain and too hurt to speak.

Scott squinted at the boys, his eyes bleary. He heard the sounds of delight from the fun they were having kicking around the makeshift puck, but he only saw the action through a hazy white film. He tried to call out but his voice got caught in his throat.

Scott rubbed his eye to try to dull the pain. It didn't help. He ran to the nearby bank of sinks and began washing his eye, but he couldn't get the sting out fast enough. He ran out of the men's locker room onto the pool deck looking for comfort. The only two lifeguards at the guard station were a guy and some girl, but they were flirting, and even though they sort of saw Scott in their periphery, they ignored him, assuming his predicament wasn't that perilous.

His eye was still burning, and of course the sweat from his fingers wasn't helping as he rubbed the white residue into his ocular area. On his way to the snack bar he passed his mother with a pair of baby twins, one a boy and one a girl, who were taking turns sucking from the same bottle. Scott's mother was preoccupied, chatting up another pool patron. Plus, the twins were a handful, so she hadn't been paying him much attention. Anger started to rise from his core. He got pissed.

When Scott reached the snack bar, he was at his wits' end. There was no relief in sight and he wasn't thinking rationally. He just had to end the stinging, right then. He grabbed a fork from the utensil caddy on the stainless steel countertop and scratched his left eye with it.

• • •

Back in the chapel Scott was almost done telling his epic flashback.

"And it hurt. But it hurt good and it eased the pain that I was feeling, and not only in the eye that was aflame from the soap. The pain soothed something else in me, deeper, that had been hurting since the twins were born and maybe even before that."

The room was awed, silent. Jaws hung open.

"Plus," Scott continued, "I really liked going to that pool. After *the incident* my mom wouldn't let me go anymore. I had to go to stupid Brown Town Hall and Recreation's dumb pool. It was all Jonathan's fault!"

Roheed interjected. "It seems like the accidental soap injury was just a catalyst and not the main root of the issue."

"Yeah, what he said," Charlie agreed. "And also, nobody told you to gouge your own eye out with a fork!"

"And you just said it was your mom who made the call about going to the pool, not Jonathan," Chris said. "So you can't honestly blame Jonathan for any of that."

Scott laughed. "Oh, but I do." He looked at Jonathan. "You ruined my life, and now I've ruined yours. *Even Stevens*, Shia LaBeouf!" Scott threw the groom wedding cake topper at Jonathan. It hit him squarely in the chest and bounced off innocuously.

Then Scott did something that, as my phone would autocorrect, really made the shirt hit the flan. He kicked over a candelabrum of still-lit candles. They scattered and flames started to lick up the ripped ribbons. The yellow carpet caught. Fire spread about the chapel.

Until then, everyone had been frozen, listening to Scott's story and then seeing what he would do. The heat unfroze them, and they sprang into action. Jonathan and Roheed began trying to stamp out the flames. Chris grabbed Tammy and escorted her to the front lobby to flee. Scott ran out of a side door that led to a back exit. Charlie followed in hot pursuit; not only was he close on Scott's tail, but it was also getting roasty-toasty in that chapel.

Charlie burst out the back door of the chapel and saw Scott hopping into Jill's car. Charlie made it to Jill's driver-side window.

"Jill?"

"Charlie," Jill said. "What's going on?"

"Drive, Jill," Scott growled from the passenger seat.

"Jill, what are you doing?" Charlie asked.

The chapel's fire alarm finally went off. Jill panicked. Her eyes wide, she mashed the gas pedal and sped off into the night. Chris, with Tammy holding onto her shoulders, caught up with Charlie. Charlie helped support Tammy. Roheed and Jonathan weren't far behind.

"There's nothing else we can do," Jonathan sighed. "We tried."

Charlie took out his phone and dialed the Yellow County Fire Department, and as Kanye once quoted Usher, "They had to let it burn." They watched as the smoke billowed, then flames appeared from the windows.

Jonathan and Chris sat on the cool grass and waited to hear the sirens that would salvage what was left of the burning chapel, knowing that no number of firemen or firewomen could save their extinguished wedding plans.

CHAPTER 16

ROHEED SLEPT ON the couch in Charlie's living room. Charlie was just curled up on the floor with his head on his pillow and his *Animaniacs* comforter wrapped around his body. They had arrived home the night before shaken—and stirred—by the events that had taken place in the chapel. Neither of them had wanted to sleep by their lonesome. Roheed had lain on the couch and Charlie silently went to get his bed things. Neither of them had even brushed their teeth, which explained why the following morning their mouths tasted like sour boogers.

A knock on the door woke them. Charlie opened just one eye and nodded for Roheed to get the door. Roheed did, begrudgingly.

It was Florence and she was glowing. She had a backpack on, she was holding her suitcase, and she was tan in a dress and the breeze blew her hair around her face like she was lit for a conditioner commercial. Roheed was a stark contrast to her effortless beauty and positive vibes. He had his version of a five o'clock shadow—a couple of unruly chin hairs that he hadn't weed-whacked with his electric razor yet. His dark mane was mostly sticking straight up on the side where his face was mashed against the pillow moments before. Nevertheless, Florence's eyes lit up; she was grinning like a goon at the site of her beau.

Roheed maintained a sober, straight face. "What's up?"

Florence was confused at Roheed's reaction to seeing her. They had been apart for weeks, she missed him, and judging by their previous FaceTimes and texts, he missed her like heck too.

"I just flew in from Florence to see you!" Florence said.

"Alabama?" Roheed asked.

"No, Italy. Haven't you gotten my messages? My texts? I've been trying to talk to you all night."

Roheed looked down at his feet. "Scott threw my phone last night."

Florence only felt more befuddled, "Why? Who? Also, what?"

Roheed's face was steely, his tone even. "This long-distance relationship is not working. It hurts too much to not be with you fully. I just realized that seeing you right now."

Florence was speechless.

Roheed continued. "You weren't here when I needed you the most. I think it's best we discontinue this relationship before we start to resent each other."

A tear tracked its way down Florence's face.

"Also, I'm assuming that you're here to surprise me and go to Jonathan and Chris's wedding with me, but the chapel burned down last night so that's probably not going to happen as planned, or in the near future at all." He began to close the door on her. "It was truly very nice to see you this one last time." He finished closing the door and turned around.

Outside that closed door, Florence folded in half, feeling like she had been stabbed in the stomach with an ice pick ironically made out of fire.

Inside that door, Roheed turned around to face Charlie, who was on the ground looking up at Roheed with wide eyes.

"That was ice cold," Charlie said.

Roheed shrugged and lay back down on the couch, facing away from Charlie. Charlie's phone rang; he was glad for the distraction. His coworker Anfernee was on the other end of the line.

"Hey, Chaz," Anfernee said.

"Hey, man."

"Timmy called out sick, can you come in, like ASAP?"

"I was supposed to have a wedding today," Charlie said out

loud, but to himself.

A smile came into Anfernee's voice. "I didn't even know you were engaged! Congrats, Chaz!"

"It wasn't *my* wedding," Charlie corrected, annoyed.

"Oh, bummer. Someday, Chaz, you'll find the right guy or girl. Anyway, can you come in?"

The light, and the hope, even the optimism that had come into Charlie's life when he first received that invitation to the wedding those couple of days ago, died. He was empty again, and uninspired, and it felt like a hundred years since those words had flowed through his fingertips even though he had written pages and pages of prose the night before. He was headed back to his job, where he would probably rise through the ranks until the company went bankrupt, and then who knew where he would end up.

He sighed and answered Anfernee with a crestfallen, "Yeah."

CHAPTER 16 1/2

SNAPSHOTS. MOMENTS IN time. Disparate, but connected.

Florence sat on a curb, wrecked, phone in hand. She scrolled until she saw Alabaster Sixx's contact info. She hesitated. Would she really call him? Now? No. She scrolled past and found Roheed's number. She called.

Charlie pulled into the Popcorn Movies parking lot. The *O*, *P*, and *C* of the backlit sign were still out. The sign still read *PORN MOVIES*.

Roheed Hitched to the airport, ignoring Armando as he tried to make small talk about what would have sounded very much like a pyramid scheme to Roheed if he had been paying full attention.

On the Yellow County Community College campus, Chris entered Jonathan's office, but Jonathan wasn't there.

Jonathan was at a Case Of The Mondays with a table of snack bar-type food in front of him. He stared at the bounty hungrily, not sure if he should dive in headfirst or abstain. He had given up snack bar food for the wedding, sure, but the wedding was essentially off, wasn't it?

Jill sat in her car outside of the burned-down chapel. Her head ached and her heart hurt.

Tammy waited to check her bags at the airport. She stood in a line that snaked around endless stanchions.

Charlie stood behind the Popcorn Movies counter in his depressing uniform. The trailer for *In Sheep's Clothing* came on the multitude of televisions that lined the walls of the store.

Roheed arrived at the airport.

On the Yellow County Community College campus Roheed's phone lay hidden by tall grass, the screen cracked and aching, ringing and ringing with Florence's image peeking through the shattered glass.

Chris sat on Jonathan's cot in his office. She looked at the Yellow County Community College Chapel's brochure. A tear fell onto the glossy paper.

Ketchup globbed onto the paper placemat in front of Jonathan as he shamefully inhaled a Case Of The Mondays burger.

Jill, in her car outside the chapel, heard a phone ringing somewhere.

Tammy sat on a bench in the airport. She sadly looked at a photo of young Jonathan and his dad. It was a candid of them at the pool. Jonathan was eating a messy popsicle; his dad had a handful of napkins. They were standing by that old trashcan that looked like a dolphin standing on its flukes.

At Popcorn Movies, the TVs were playing the trailer for *In Sheep's Clothing* again. Charlie ran around the store, frenetic, manic, arms full of remotes, trying to turn off the screens with little success. A TV over yonder would turn off, and then over there one would turn back on. He unplugged TVs and switched off power strips.

At the airport, Roheed bought a ticket back west. One way. He had made sure to shave his scraggly facial hair. Sadly, being clean-shaven helped the whole airport process go a little smoother.

In Jonathan's office, Chris ripped up the brochure and let it fall to the floor, the pieces of torn paper drifting like the ashes in the smoky air the night before.

At COTM, Jonathan was a mess. He was covered in nacho cheese and ketchup and spicy mustard, yellow mustard, and honey mustard—an artist's palette of condiments, a Pollock of sauces. The server approached nervously. Jonathan motioned for her to keep it coming with his pointer finger rotating clockwise but off kilter in the air. If she were a bartender serving booze, she would have cut him off, but since she was merely a server of fatty food, she turned around and headed back into the kitchen for more calorie-containing vittles.

There was still one television left on in Popcorn Movies, mocking Charlie with the *In Sheep's Clothing* trailer once again. Charlie grabbed a stanchion from the impulse aisle and ran toward the TV in slow motion. He didn't actually run in slow motion, but it seemed like it to Anfernee, who admittedly was a little tripped out on the meds he had taken earlier to quell his cough. Charlie threw the stanchion like a javelin and it smashed the TV's screen.

At the airport, Roheed waited in line at security.

On campus, near the ashy guts of the chapel, Jill scrambled on her hands and knees in the tall grass looking for the source of the ringing. She found Roheed's phone and picked it up. She carefully answered the phone, avoiding the broken glass of the cracked screen. "Hello?" she said cautiously.

At first Florence was confused, but she registered who had answered and listened intently.

Jill knelt in the weeds, pouring herself into the phone.

Florence nodded fervently. She ended the call and dialed a new number.

Jill was back in her car. Shift, foot to gas, tires peel.

Fade to black.

CHAPTER 17

CHARLIE STOOD IN the aftermath of his television destruction. The floor of Popcorn Movies was littered with television remotes and shattered glass from the broken TV. The impulse aisle stanchions were all overturned. Anfernee stood there, mouth open wide. Charlie's phone rang in his pocket.

"Hello?" he answered. He listened for a moment, nodded his head as if the person on the other end of the line could hear his head rattle, and then ended the call.

Anfernee gestured to the carnage. "Brah!"

Charlie shrugged. "I quit."

"I'm not mad at ya, Chaz," Anfernee said.

Charlie stepped lightly over the sharp shards and exited. Driving away from that place, Charlie felt free. He sort of wondered if there were going to be repercussions for harpooning a big hunk of metal at a TV set, but he figured they could keep his last paycheck, or whatever. He was never going back there.

Charlie drove past the Case Of The Mondays that was on the other side of Greenbelt Road from Popcorn Movies. Inside, Jonathan was about to slam dunk a fistful of chicken fingers into the dip cup of BBQ sauce, but his phone rang so he set down the poultry's phalanges and answered it. His eyes went wide. He took a bunch of money out of his wallet, left it on the table, and bolted.

Miles away, Roheed had his shoes off in the line for security at the airport. His carry-on items were stuffed into a grey tray, ready for the conveyor belt. He was already picturing returning to the West Coast, getting some sleep, finishing up the paperwork on the sale of his app, and starting over. It hurt his heart but he felt that if he could get through the initial stages of mourning the loss of his relationship with Florence, that eventually he would be okay. He was practical in that way. But then he thought about the time he had spent with Florence, that first summer when their love had sparked a little fire that had grown and been burning ever since. He hardened his emotions. He was getting on the plane. It was over.

A tap on his shoulder rocked him out of his thoughts. It was Tammy. She was on the phone. She gestured to it and said, "Florence." She handed him the phone. Roheed was surprised, so surprised that he walked out of the security line with his tray of carry-on items. His socked feet padded out of the airport with Tammy as he listened to the voice on the other end of the call.

Jill knocked on a door. She rang the doorbell and knocked again. June Summers opened the door, confused. June, of course, was the board member who had given Charlie, Roheed, Jill, and the rest of the snack bar crew such a hard time the summer that Bill had died. She had caught Jonathan living in the Yellow County Community Swim and Racquet Club guard office. She had also been secretly rooting for Brown Town Hall and Recreation to win the Tri-County Relay Race because her twins, Channan and Shannon Twinsley—their father's last name—were members of the Brown Town Swim Team.

Jill explained what she was doing there at June's house. She talked too fast, but June listened intently. June called back into her house. Her other son, who was none other than Scott, the dude with the eye, whose last name happened to be Summers, appeared. June questioned him about the events of the night before, and he nodded sheepishly. June was appalled. The cops hadn't caught up to Scott yet, but she told him that she was sure they would sooner rather than later and that he would be in a whole heap of trouble.

Chris was still sitting on Jonathan's cot, contemplating their ruined wedding, wondering if they should just cut their losses and go to the Yellow County Courthouse to sign whatever papers and just be done with it. But then Jonathan darkened the doorway. Chris looked up. Jonathan was grinning. He was wearing an old Yellow County Community Swim and Racquet Club T-shirt, size *M*, just right. He reached out his hand. She took it.

Jonathan and Chris walked out of the building onto the lush quad. Judas was waiting for them in his Hummer H2. As Judas drove, Jonathan and Chris sat in the back, Jonathan's arm around Chris. Chris watched out the window.

"Where are we going?" Chris asked.

But Jonathan didn't answer and he didn't need to. The roads and the trees and the sights became familiar to Chris and she got choked up and tears began to slip 'n slide down her cheeks, but she was smiling through them.

• • •

It was late afternoon by the time Judas's H2 pulled into the Yellow County Community Swim and Racquet Club parking lot. Charlie and Roheed were there; Charlie still in his Popcorn Movies uniform, Roheed still with no shoes on. Florence and Jill were there, and Tammy. Also in attendance were June and Scott Summers, and the Twinsley twins. Kenneth Strangleman was there too, as well as Devon Wilkenshire, who had been called to come unlock the guard gate. He had obliged and given his blessing to what was about to go down. Judas parked diagonally across all of the disabled person parking spots, because that's the kind of D-bag he was and would forever be, even in a moment like this. He and Jonathan and Chris exited the car. The small crowd cheered.

"What's going on?" Chris whispered to Jonathan.

"I'm not sure," he replied. "But let's just go with it."

Chris smiled at Jonathan. She hugged him close. She knew whatever was happening on the pool grounds was probably positive. She felt secure holding Jonathan's arm; they were a team. She would have followed—or led for that matter—him into battle.

Florence walked Jonathan and Chris into the Yellow County Community Swim and Racquet Club. It was sparsely but beautifully decorated for their wedding. Someone had hastily scrawled *Poole-Partee* on a piece of cardboard and lashed it to a guard umbrella. Blue-and-white-striped deck chairs lined the pool's twelve-foot deep well area. The racing flags usually used at swim meets were strung like garlands around the high and low diving boards. Classical music played over the pool's PA system. Chris's dads were there, setting up the last of the decorations.

Jonathan covered his mouth with his hand, taking in the majesty. "Oh, wow," he said quietly, humbled.

Chris just let it go, she cried and smiled and shook her head in disbelief. She waved to her dads, and they waved back.

"This is our wedding," she said to Jonathan. "We found it."

Jonathan squeezed her close, and said, simply, "Yeah," because if he would have said anything more, his voice would have cracked with emotion.

CHAPTER 18

IT WAS MAGIC hour. Judas was officiating the wedding. He stood with Jonathan and Chris atop the high dive, speaking loudly into a plastic lifeguard megaphone. The rest of the party sat down on the pool deck in those blue-and-white chairs by the well.

". . . And by the power vested in me," Judas said in his best brotivational speaker voice, "by the online course I took earlier this afternoon, and the great County of Yellow, I now pronounce you husband and wife."

Jonathan and Chris kissed, passionately, for a while, like get-a-room-already long. When they finished, Chris kept her lips close to Jonathan's ear.

"I know that you wish that Bill could be here," she said quietly.

"Yeah," Jonathan agreed.

"And your dad," Chris said.

Jonathan nodded.

Chris continued, "But now you have two dads too."

Jonathan looked down from their perch atop the high dive and saw Chris's dads. They were holding each other, caught up in the moment. Jonathan smiled, his eyes wet.

"Ladies and gentleman," Judas orated, "It is with GREAT pleasure that I present to you, Jonathan and Christmas Poole-

Partee. Mr. and Mrs. Poole-Partee, you may do your first cannonball as husband and wife."

Roheed leaned over to Charlie. "Did you know Chris's full name is Christmas?"

"No I did not," Charlie replied. "Christmas Partee, what a badass name."

Roheed agreed.

Jonathan and Chris smiled, clasped hands, and did a wicked double cannonball off the high dive, splashing their guests in their chairs. Everyone cheered.

Music started playing over the PA again and Jonathan and Chris went to go change into dry clothes and everyone of age started drinking and celebrating.

A little later, Jonathan and Chris hightailed it to the shuffleboard court that had been MacGrubered into a dance floor. They looked across the way and nodded to Chris's dads, who were cutting a rug themselves. Judas danced with Shannon Twinsley, who kept looking longingly across the pool deck to Channan, who was dancing with their mom, June. The creepy twins wanted to dance with each other in a not-so-familial way.

Roheed caught Florence's eye. She walked over and met him by the waterslide. They looked out over the softly shimmering pool. Light danced in the water's reflection.

"This is incredible," Roheed said. Now that Florence was close, he couldn't make his eyes meet hers.

Florence nodded. "All it took was a couple of phone calls and some elbow grease. Turns out a lot of people really love Jonathan and Chris."

It was Roheed's turn to nod. There was an awkward silence for a few moments. Florence looked down at the concrete.

"I'm really sorry about what I said earlier," Roheed broke the silence. Florence looked up at him. Finally, their eyes met. Roheed continued, "I want to be with you, but I don't want to be with you and apart from you."

"I understand," Florence said. She did; she agreed, and she felt it, too.

"I need to be on the West Coast until next summer, when my app launches, so I suppose that we must take a break or break up," Roheed said sadly.

"We don't," Florence answered, her face looking like it had been harboring a rogue smile for several seconds.

"We don't?" Roheed said, shocked.

Florence let her smile free and gushed. "Jerd McKinley just sold a new *Rich B Words* show, *Rich B Words of Orange County*. They're moving the entire original cast to Laguna Beach! They're hoping it's going to be bigger than that one reality show that was filmed in Laguna Beach—I forget what it was called right now."

"That's incredible!" Roheed said, feeling like his life had been doomed but a last-minute call from the governor had sprung him.

"We'll be a quick plane ride away, and I'm sure my shooting schedule won't be too intense. I can stay with you whenever we're not filming."

Roheed couldn't contain himself. "May I kiss you?" he asked.

Florence rolled her eyes and smiled. "You don't need to ask me that every time." She hardly got the word "time" out because Roheed planted a big sloppy one right on her smackeroonie. Roheed cupped the back of Florence's neck in his surprisingly strong hand and the whole thing was pretty hot.

"Wow!" Roheed needed to catch his breath after that one. Then he remembered, "Hey, speaking of Jerd, you need to talk to Charlie about *In Sheep's Clothing*."

"Jerd told me that Charlie was taken care of," Florence said. Roheed shook his head. Florence immediately took out her phone and walked away from the pool to make the call. Roheed let her leave, still looking wistfully at the pool's gentle water. Then he decided to head up to the snack bar.

Charlie manned—*personned* as he called it—the grill, sweating, flipping burgers, and rolling dogs. He was setting up large trays of snack bar food to cater the wedding. Roheed entered the bar.

"Glad to see you buddy," Charlie said. "I have wieners that need bunning."

Roheed slid into his sidekick role effortlessly. He put hot dogs into lightly toasted hot dog buns.

"Did you talk to Jill?" Roheed asked.

Charlie shook his head.

"You should probably straighten things out with her,"

Roheed said. "There's a high probability that she wasn't working as Scott's wheelperson in a planned arson."

"No, I know," Charlie said. "I already talked about everything with Scott. He came and apologized and offered to help so I gave him a pretty terrible job."

Scott appeared from around the corner, a poorly made chicken quesadilla on a plate in his hand. "They're so hard to make," he griped.

"That one's not good enough, Scott," Charlie barked, "Start over. And make sure all of the fifty chicken quesadillas we need for this party are perfect!"

"But there aren't even fifty people here," Scott complained.

For once Charlie gave Scott the evil eye. Scott grumbled.

"And he's going to turn himself in for burning down the chapel," Charlie said to Roheed, and then turned. "Right, Scott?"

"I'd rather face the Yellow County sheriff than my mom," Scott assured Roheed.

Roheed nodded. He was sure that June could be a big *B* word when she wanted to, and also when she didn't want to, and also always.

Charlie took off his *Kiss the Cook . . . Please!!!?!* apron and hung it around Roheed's neck. "Show him how it's done," he told Roheed.

Roheed regarded the apron with reverence, then turned to Scott and began the chicken quesadilla-making tutorial to end all chicken quesadilla-making tutorials. Like, if you were to search "chicken quesadilla-making tutorial" on YouTube, you would want the chicken quesadilla-making tutorial that Roheed gave to Scott.

Jill sat on the pool deck, her feet dangling in the water. Charlie sat next to her. Jill's heart was racing; she had been nervous about this conversation all day. Her words flowed like an inner-city fire hydrant on a hot day. "It wasn't what it looked like. I was scared."

Charlie stopped her. "I talked to Scott, I know everything," he said, and he kissed her and the soft music kept playing over the PA and people were dancing. All of the sudden, Judas popped champagne and there was cheering as he drank it straight from the bottle and jumped off the high dive. Fireworks erupted from the sand volleyball court, lighting up the sky in the shapes of doggies and ducks and dolphins, their reflections dancing on the pool's surface.

Charlie and Jill stopped kissing momentarily, "Did *you* know Chris was short for Christmas?" Charlie asked.

"Nope," Jill smiled. "It's cute, though."

"Totally," Charlie agreed, and they went back to making out, Charlie's webbed toes swaying in the water next to Jill's petite footsies. The waves their feet made spread out across the pool and turned into ripples that eventually turned into nothing.

EPILOGUE

IT WAS LATE.

The Poole-Partee wedding was beautiful from top to bottom, stem to stern, but the evening had to end at some point for fear of pissing off the lingering moon, and you don't want to get on that dude's dark side.

"Sorry again for ruining your wedding," Scott said sheepishly, taking his leave.

Chris looked at Jonathan. "You didn't," Jonathan told him.

Scott walked away humbly. June flounced over.

"I'm glad I'm actually seeing you in person after all the emails you haven't returned," she said to Jonathan.

"Emails?" Jonathan was confused.

"Are you confused about what I just said, or the existence of emails in general?" June said impatiently.

"I didn't know I had an email. Does it go to my work computer?" Jonathan was a little behind the times.

June continued, hoping that Chris would pick up the slack. "I need to correspond with the majority owner of the pool sometimes, you know, and you've been making that very difficult."

Jonathan's face was still as blank as the check in that '90s movie about the kid with the blank check; you know, *Rookie of the Year*.

June shook her head. "You really don't know what I'm talking about?"

He didn't.

"You still own 51 percent of the pool—Bill left you the majority stake of the club in his will," June exclaimed. Jonathan and Chris were shocked. June continued, "You couldn't live on the pool grounds, but I can't steal the pool away from you, as much as I'd like to."

"I just assumed . . ." Jonathan began. "I don't know what I assumed."

"Well, you know what happens when you assume," June said. "You make an ass out of *you—rself.*"

"Wow," Chris said, looking around the pool.

"Board meetings are at the Yellow County Community Center on the second Tuesday of every month except November and December. That's when basketball season begins, and the Yellow County Yellow Yellow Jackets have practices on Tuesdays. I expect you to start showing up."

"To the Yellow Jackets' practices?" Jonathan said. "I haven't played in years, but I guess it's true what they say, ball is life."

June opened her mouth to respond when she realized that Jonathan was joking and flashing a sly grin.

"I'll be at the meetings," Jonathan assured June.

She harrumphed and walked away. Jonathan just looked at Chris and laughed. Chris shook her head.

Over yonder, Charlie, Jill, Roheed, Florence, and Judas sat in the gazebo. Jill sat on Charlie's lap, Roheed and Florence were snuggled up, and Judas was lightly caressing his boo, a bottle of champagne.

"I couldn't get Jerd on the phone," Florence said.

"Typical," Charlie scoffed.

"But I'll be seeing him a ton once I'm out in Orange County," Florence said hopefully.

"Tell him I hope he likes spending my money," Charlie said caustically. The *In Sheep's Clothing* premiere date was quickly approaching. Charlie was bummed. There was nothing he could do.

"You should go out there and confront him," Jill said.

"What?" Charlie started, "No. . ."

"Yeah!" Jill said.

Florence was on board. "I can set it all up, it'll be easy. And you have documents and emails and everything I'm sure."

"I guess," Charlie said cautiously.

"You should do it, bro," Judas added.

"I guess I did just quit my job," Charlie said, sort of to himself because he was the only person who still needed convincing at that point. Then he looked at Jill. "But what about us?" he asked earnestly.

Jill laughed. Charlie was confused. She saw his reaction and stopped laughing. "Oh, you're serious?" she said. "I didn't know we were an *us*, I mean, I did just have a very fun, wish fulfilling long-weekend fling with you, but *us*, I don't know about all that."

"Wow!" Charlie murmured.

"We can figure that stuff out later," Jill said. "You need to go stop that movie before it comes out without your name on it."

"Damn!" Charlie huffed. "I mean shoot, I don't have anything holding me down here."

Judas looked around excitedly. "Does this mean what I think it means?"

Charlie smiled. "I guess I'm going to LA?"

"Hell yeah!" Judas said.

Roheed was feeling frisky. "Hell yes!" he added.

Charlie laughed. Judas passed him the bottle of champagne and he took a big swig, wondering what he had just gotten himself into and hoping that he would have the nerve to follow through, even when the booze wore off the next day.

• • •

Chris and Jonathan finally made it back to Chris's house eventually, which now, Jonathan guessed, was *their* house. He carried Chris over the threshold. He flicked the light on with his free hand.

"I'm excited to have some hot, steamy, post-marital intercourse," Jonathan said, joking but serious.

"Me, too," Chris smiled.

Jonathan hurried them to the bedroom. He set Chris's legs down but didn't let her go just yet. They kissed passionately.

"Jonathan?" Chris said through the kisses.

"Mhm," he mumbled.

"Do you like the new furniture?" Chris said coyly.

Jonathan glanced around the room, his lips still locked to Chris's, but then he noticed something and his eyes widened and his mouth stopped kissing.

"Jonathan," Chris began, and Jonathan didn't respond.

There was a brand-new crib sitting in the corner of the room.

"You're going to be a daddy."